Moonlight

Moonlight is another in the OTHER WORLD series, which brings you the best in fantasy, horror, magic, the supernatural and science fiction. Also in this series are *October Moon*, *Gemini Game* and *House of the Dead* by well-known writer Michael Scott.

Watch out for the OTHER WORLD logo, and prepare to be chilled and thrilled!

Michael Carroll

Michael Carroll is twenty-seven years old and has already
had many incarnations – as postman, computer program-
mer, sci-fi addict and now as writer. He lives in Dublin
and is a former chairman of the Irish Science Fiction
Association and co-founder of the humour magazine *PFJ*.
His story *On Glory Roads of Pure Delight* won the Aisling
Gheal Award for Best Original Fantasy Story of 1992.

About this book

"*Moonlight* has its own special magic to spellbind a young
reader, and a young-old one too. A very well-considered
starting point, an admirable heroine and some fair dra-
matics make this novel a grand read ... most enjoyable, a
thoroughly engrossing read."

Anne McCaffrey

Moonlight

MICHAEL CARROLL

THE O'BRIEN PRESS

DUBLIN

First published 1993 by The O'Brien Press Ltd.,
20 Victoria Road, Dublin 6, Ireland.

Copyright © Michael Carroll 1993
British Library Cataloguing-in-publication Data
A catalogue reference for this title is available
from the British Library.

10 9 8 7 6 5 4 3 2 1

ISBN 0 – 86278 –354-2

The O'Brien Press receives assistance from
The Arts Council/An Chomhairle Ealaíon

Typesetting and layout: The O'Brien Press
Cover illustration: Katharine White
Cover design: Neasa Ní Chianáin
Colour separations: Lithoset, Dublin
Printing: Cox & Wyman Ltd., Reading

For my friend and mentor –
the Bard of Ireland, Michael Scott

CHAPTER I

It was science that started it all.
Science put the tracking satellites into orbit, enabled their computers and communications to work, and gave people the ability to see and understand far beyond normal senses.

Since the industrial revolution, the earth has been growing steadily warmer, and this global warming often has severe side effects.

The computer-enhanced satellite pictures of the melting Norwegian glacier seemed normal enough at first, but a sharp-eyed computer operator noticed the dark patch buried deep in the glacier. The glacier was just west of Nordkapp, the northernmost tip of the country, well into the Arctic circle.

Glaciers are not simply huge slabs of ice ... They are formed over hundreds, even thousands of years, layer upon layer of crushed snow and ice, picking up pulverised rocks and dirt as they move and grow.

It's rare that the frozen carcass of an animal is found, so the dark spot in the Norwegian glacier caused something of a minor international media interest.

Ψ   Ψ   Ψ

Out of the corner of her eye, Cathy Donnelly watched her Aunt Margaret getting ready for a night on the town. They lived in an old two-bedroomed flat in the heart of Dublin, though Margaret preferred to call it an apartment.

Cathy was thirteen, and though her aunt was almost three times her age, Margaret bounced giddily around the flat like a teenager.

"How do I look?" Margaret asked.

Cathy looked up. Like a woman pretending to be ten years younger, she thought. But she knew better than to say something like that out loud. She put on her best smile. "You look great!"

Thrilled with herself, Margaret grabbed her jacket and bag. "I'm late. I said I'd meet Dave at eight!" She walked towards the door, then stopped and looked back, frowning. "I'll be back around eleven. You're to be in bed by then. Have you tidied your room?"

Cathy sighed. Here we go, she said to herself. I knew her good mood was too good to last. "Yes, I tidied my room."

"Well, run the hoover over this place. And don't forget to dry the dishes."

"It's not my turn!"

Margaret crossed her arms and tapped her foot. "Would it hurt if for once you did a little extra around the house? Would it kill you to get off your backside? You know I haven't got the time tonight."

Cathy glared at her aunt. "That's funny, you said the

same thing last night, and it was your turn then too!"

Margaret checked that she had her keys, then opened the door. "Just do it!"

She slammed the door behind her.

Ψ   Ψ   Ψ

By the time she'd finished the housework, Cathy was too tired to read. She turned on the TV and watched the nine o'clock news with the usual boredom. It was the same old bad news: politicians arguing, oil prices up, terrorist attacks and an increase in unemployment figures.

Even though school was over for the summer, Cathy wasn't allowed out after seven in the evenings. Margaret was very strict on the matter: she was usually going out with some boyfriend or other and didn't want to have to be worried about Cathy.

Cathy didn't like her aunt very much, and she knew that the feeling went both ways, but they were stuck with each other, and Cathy didn't have any choice but to do as she was told.

Her father had died before she was born, and her mother was killed in a car crash when Cathy was only four, so she'd been raised by her grandparents. Now, however, her grandparents had gone to live in England, where Grandad's retirement money, combined with the little they had saved and the money they got from selling their house, allowed them to buy a small cottage in Cornwall, where Cathy's grandmother had grown up.

Margaret O'Toole had reluctantly agreed to look after

9

her niece, though Cathy knew that her aunt resented the intrusion on her life. Margaret's flat was on the top floor of an old five-storey house in Dublin's Temple Bar, an area that was now trendy and rapidly becoming expensive. Margaret spent much of the time wishing she had bought the flat when she'd had the chance a few years ago, because now it was worth at least three times as much.

Cathy had spent an entire, tearful weekend saying goodbye to her friends in Waterford. That had been four months ago, and she'd hadn't made any new friends yet. She wrote to her grandparents a lot: being locked up at night she didn't have much else to do with her time.

So while her friends in Waterford were all meeting in each other's houses, playing records and having pyjama parties, Cathy sat in her aunt's flat in Dublin and read or watched the television.

She was lonely. She hated her life, and couldn't wait until she was old enough to move out and get a place of her own. She decided she'd leave when she was sixteen, but that meant three more years ...

So she stayed in at night and watched television. Only one news item caught her attention that night. The dead animal in the Norwegian glacier had been cut free and examined by several noted biologists and experts on prehistoric animals, who were filmed standing around in thick padded anoraks and trying to look intelligent in front of the cameras.

The animal had proved to be a badly decomposed and mutilated horse. The experts guessed that it was at least ten thousand years old, though they'd need to perform extensive tests to be certain. The beast's head had been removed, and there was some speculation that this had been done as part of an ancient ritual.

Cathy felt sorry for the horse.

ψ   ψ   ψ

Roger Brannigan was also watching the same news report. He was in the sittingroom of his five-bedroomed home in County Dublin, in a leather-covered reclining armchair that cost almost a thousand pounds, in front of a huge state-of-the-art wide-screen television set.

Brannigan was forty-five, though he played a lot of squash and looked a good ten years younger. He also rode a lot: his house was on the edge of the fifteen-acre stud farm that he owned, and though Brannigan could have his pick of the twenty-three horses, he rarely bothered about most of them. His favourite was a four-year-old mare nicknamed Misty, and though making money was Brannigan's full-time obsession, he'd resisted all offers for Misty.

All his life he'd been fascinated with horses. He could usually tell, just by looking at a day-old foal, whether it would ever be a winner.

And his horses were bred to be winners. He had commissioned a computer program that, given the complete history of a mare and stallion, could predict with reasonable accuracy the abilities of the offspring. However, real life never completely matched the computer's guesses, and it always cheered Brannigan up when the computer got it wrong.

The news item on the preserved horse hit Roger Brannigan like a wet hammer. Suppose, he said to himself, just suppose that ten thousand years ago horses were faster, stronger ...

What if that strain of horse could be brought back?

He smiled to himself, and reached for the phone. He knew just the person who could do it.

Ψ   Ψ   Ψ

Dr Emil Feyerman was tall and thin, with a shock of grey hair, and was in his late fifties. He was the sort of scientist that everyone expected would wear thick glasses and speak with a strong German accent. However, his eyesight was almost perfect and his accent was pure mid-Atlantic: not really American, but not really European either.

Feyerman was a specialist in genetic research, and had made a small fortune working for people like Roger Brannigan, examining their race horses and mating them to produce superior offspring. It was he who had written Brannigan's prized computer program, and Feyerman had been paid a quarter of a million Irish pounds for it.

He always smiled when he thought of Brannigan's gullibility. All Feyerman had done was to modify a simple computer-dating program. After all, he had reasoned, Brannigan just wants his horses to find the right mate.

He modified the program to do simple matching of DNA patterns, the genetic codes that shape the growth and attributes of every animal.

In most animals, the female produces an egg with half of its DNA pattern in the form of chromosomes, the male produces sperm with the missing half, and these combine to form offspring containing attributes of both parents.

Very early after conception, the foetus's DNA determines which of the chromosomes is dominant, so certain traits such as red hair or green eyes are carried from one generation to the next. Occasionally the DNA gives unexpected results, a pair of tabby cats could produce a grey kitten, a "throw-back" to an ancestor that could have been several generations in the past.

Feyerman had analysed the DNA samples of hundreds of different horses, and was now able to tell which strains of DNA could be combined for the best results.

What he really wanted to do was clone the best horses, and – in theory – this could be done from a single blood cell. Each cell contained the DNA structure for the entire horse, and, given complete understanding of the DNA and enough equipment, Feyerman hoped that one day the animals could be grown in a laboratory, in artificial wombs.

The clone would be an exact copy of the original horse, or even better. If the DNA structure could be improved upon, there was no reason a laboratory-born horse couldn't be even more efficient.

Of course, Feyerman wasn't foolish enough to think

that such a thing would be achieved in his own lifetime. Though he was easily the best in his field, he knew that he was as far from being able to clone a horse as the alchemists of old had been from turning lead into gold.

But there was a sort of middle ground. For decades farm animals had been artificially inseminated, where the sperm from the male was placed into the female by mechanical means, allowing the farmer to select an appropriate mate to produce pigs that gave better, leaner pork, or cows that could yield better milk.

Artificial insemination was very common in horse-breeding, often foals were born to a mare that had never even seen the stallion. But if the unfertilised egg of a mare was to be modified to contain a complete set of the mare's chromosomes, and the egg placed back into the mare, the foal could be an exact copy of its mother.

This, too, had yet to be achieved, though Feyerman knew he was close to success. The difficulty lay in modifying the unfertilised egg.

And that led to another difficulty. The money he'd received from Brannigan was almost gone.

So when the phone rang, and Brannigan spoke of his idea to reintroduce the extinct strain of horse, Feyerman was thrilled.

He kept calm and tutted and sucked in his breath, the way a mechanic will when he's just about to tell you that you can't get the parts anymore, and it'll cost you.

They discussed the idea that the dead horse's body might contain some frozen, but undamaged, cells. It was an attractive concept, that a horse that died over ten thousand years ago could still produce children.

Feyerman and Brannigan finally agreed on a price of one million pounds, payable half now, and half on success.

The scientist knew that the publicity alone would generate Brannigan much more than a million, but he didn't mind. Success in this venture would earn him a Nobel prize, at the very least.

ψ   ψ   ψ

Back in her aunt's flat in Dublin, Cathy Donnelly watched the ten o'clock news to see if there was another report about the prehistoric horse.

There was something important about this, but she wasn't sure exactly what it was, or even how she knew.

Somehow, Cathy sensed that her life was going to change.

And deep down, in the back of her mind, she realised that the discovery of the decapitated horse was eventually going to change the life of every person on the planet.

CHAPTER II

By the end of their first year together, Cathy and Margaret had long since stopped talking to each other. Cathy concluded that relatives aren't naturally friends, and decided that it would be best just to keep out of her way.

At first, she'd made every effort to become friends with Margaret, but the older woman just wasn't interested. Margaret's boyfriend Dave was long gone, as were the three others in the past year.

Cathy knew that Margaret blamed her for her unstable love life. "No sane man wants a thirteen-year-old girl acting as a chaperon!" Margaret had said. "You keep getting in the way!"

The morning of Cathy's fourteenth birthday, the first thought that occurred to her was: only two more years to go. It was with that thought that she realised she truly hated living with her aunt.

True, Margaret looked after Cathy, fed her and clothed her, but she made Cathy's life a misery. It's like having an older sister from Hell, Cathy thought.

Margaret still hardly let Cathy out of the flat, so Cathy

took every chance she could to get away. She spent a lot of time browsing through the second-hand bookshop on Aungier Street, but it wasn't enough. She wanted to meet people.

One day, towards the end of the school year, she spotted an ad for a summer job looking after the horses on a stud farm. She didn't know much about horses, but she thought that it wouldn't hurt to apply.

A letter from the farm arrived a week later, saying that the job had been given to someone else, but that they'd keep her letter on file in case something else cropped up in the future. Cathy was bitterly disappointed, and sulked for the rest of the day.

Two days later, Cathy was chatting to old Mr Nicholls, a neighbour who always seemed quite content to sit on his steps and talk to anybody who happened to be passing. She told him about not getting the job on the stud farm, and he just grinned when she mentioned the name of the farm, and said, "Don't you worry, Cathy, leave it to me!"

The following day there was a phone call from the farm secretary offering Cathy a Saturday job, if she was still interested. The secretary said that Cathy had been recommended by Mr Nicholls, who was a good friend of the family that owned the farm before Roger Brannigan bought it.

Cathy ran next door to thank Mr Nicholls, and admitted that she felt guilty about getting a job because of someone she knew, rather than on her own merit. But Mr

Nicholls smiled and told her that these days that was how everyone got a job.

The farm was almost ten miles away, right on the edge of the county, almost into Wicklow, but Mr Nicholls offered to drive her down on the first morning. He said that he had business in Wicklow, and would be going that direction anyway.

Cathy fidgeted nervously during the drive. She was worried that she wouldn't be up to the job, and hadn't a clue what was expected of her.

"Don't worry about a thing," Mr Nicholls said as the car pulled to a stop outside the gates. "Just be yourself, and if they're not happy with you, then that's their loss."

Cathy smiled at him, and tried to look braver than she felt. "Thanks again, Mr Nicholls. You're very kind."

After the old man had waved goodbye and driven away, Cathy stood staring at the gates for more than a minute before she built up enough courage to go in. She took a deep breath, then held her head high and strode through the gates as though she'd worked there all her life.

The stud farm was called Lowlands, the name arched across the gateposts in ornate lettering. The gate led directly into a courtyard, on the left was the manager's office and reception, and ahead and to the right were old stables converted into offices. There were narrow lanes leading away at the corners of the courtyard.

Several large cars were parked in the courtyard, but only one stood out. It was a brand new BMW, registered in

Dublin. Cathy looked at it and nodded. The owner's car, she said to herself. It has to be.

As she looked around, three men left the manager's office and strode towards the farthest lane. One of them glanced around and noticed Cathy. He told the others to go on.

"And who might you be?" He was tall and slim, with thick, closely cropped black hair, and a boyish grin that really made Cathy feel welcome.

Cathy took a deep breath. "I'm Cathy Donnelly. I'm supposed to start work here today."

"I'm Damian Corscadden," he said, shaking her hand. "I'm your boss, but don't worry, I'm not *too* much of a slave-driver." He smiled again.

"I'm afraid I don't know very much about horses," Cathy said.

Damian looked around at her. "Well, come with me. You're about to get your first lesson."

They hurried to catch up with the other two men. Damian didn't introduce them to Cathy, and they didn't seem to notice her. They passed a row of ten stables, and entered a large shed.

From the smell, Cathy guessed that it too was being used as a stable, and she was right. A mare was sitting on a thick bed of dirty straw, and she appeared to be asleep. Her coat was matted with straw and dirt, and from what Cathy could see by squinting into the darkness, the mare was heavily pregnant.

The two men continued talking.

"This isn't right, Emil," the shorter and better dressed one said. "What is it? A coma?"

The other man shrugged. "Not at all. Everything indicates that she's asleep."

"She's much too quiet."

"She's fine, Roger. Take my word for it."

"How much time has she got?"

"About a month. I'll be back a week before then."

"What if she goes early?"

Emil Feyerman shrugged. "She won't."

"How can you be so sure?"

Feyerman laughed. "It's my job to be sure. Just make certain that she's well looked after."

Roger Brannigan looked around, and noticed Cathy for the first time.

"This is Cathy," Damian said. "She's just started today."

Brannigan nodded. "Good, good. Well, you'll show her what to do, eh?"

Damian nodded. "I thought we'd start with the feeding, then on to mucking out and grooming."

The horse opened her eyes and looked around. She shuffled a bit, pulling her forelegs closer under her. Cathy stepped forward, and the horse tilted her head gently in her direction.

Feyerman looked from the horse to Cathy. "You've never been this close to a horse before, have you?"

My God, Cathy thought, am I going to be fired already? She swallowed. "Well, not really."

The man nodded. "I thought not. Misty here is in a funny sort of mood. She won't let any of the regulars look at her, but she's got no problem with you being here." He frowned thoughtfully for a few moments. "School is over for the summer, yes?"

Cathy nodded.

"Good." He turned to Brannigan. "Misty can sense that there's something different about her pregnancy. She's alienating herself from the other beasts. She smells them on the other workers, but not on ... " He paused, and looked at Damian.

"Cathy," Damian said. "Cathy Donnelly."

Feyerman nodded absently. "Yes. Cathy. Perhaps we could have her here till the birth."

Brannigan nodded. "Good idea. Would you like that, Cathy? Looking after Misty until her foal is born? As soon as you can, come here and look after her full time. You'll be well-paid, and you won't have to worry about somewhere to stay. There's a sort of guest room out front."

Cathy didn't have to think about it for long. "I'll do it."

"How soon can you start?"

Cathy paused. "Tomorrow?"

Brannigan and Feyerman smiled at her, asked Damian to make the arrangements, and abruptly walked away.

Damian and Cathy watched them go. "That was quick," he said with a smile. "Some girls would give their right arm for a chance like that."

Cathy shrugged. "So. Where do we start?"

The young man looked around the large shed. "Right. This is a wall. This is the floor. That big brown thing with the tail is a horse."

"Slow down," Cathy said. "I'll have to take notes."

Damian laughed. "Let's see if we can get her onto her feet."

He reached forward and patted Misty on the neck, but the horse turned away from him. He stepped back. "You want to have a go?"

Cathy looked at the horse's deep brown eyes. She understands, Cathy said to herself. She knows that I won't harm her.

She walked up to Misty and placed her hand on the horse's neck. She was surprised at how warm Misty was. Cathy ran her hand along the horse's back. "She's beautiful."

Damian nodded. "She's a four-year-old thoroughbred racehorse," he said. "She cost more than either of us will ever see in our lives."

Cathy patted Misty on the rump. "Come on, Misty. See if you can stand. Come on, up! Up!"

Misty whinnied quietly, then slowly pushed herself up to her feet. She was much bigger than Cathy had imagined.

The horse turned her head to Cathy and nuzzled her.

Damian whistled. "You know, that's the first time she's done anything anyone has asked for weeks. See if you can lead her out."

Cathy put her hand up to Misty's mouth, and laughed

as the horse gently nibbled her fingers. Cathy stepped back, heading for the door, and Misty followed obediently.

"Okay," Damian said. "Now leave her out there and come on back."

She patted Misty again. "Stay there, I'll be back."

Inside, Damian had grabbed a wheelbarrow and a shovel. "Get the other shovel," he said. "This is the hard part."

"What are we going to do?"

The young man smiled, and nodded towards the dirty straw and piles of horse dung on the ground. "What do you think?"

Ψ Ψ Ψ

In the house, Roger Brannigan and Emil Feyerman went over their charts.

"You're certain that everything is okay?" Brannigan asked.

"Will you stop asking me that! Yes! Everything's fine!"

Brannigan sighed. "We should have tried this with the cell of a live horse first."

"I know what I'm doing," Feyerman said. "Besides, would you rather have waited another year to find out what our prehistoric horse looks like?"

"I hope you're right about the dominant chromosomes."

"I am right. It's my job."

Brannigan leaned back and put his feet up on his desk.

"I've been thinking about this a lot, Emil. What if the beast doesn't eat normal food? Maybe it lived on something else."

"Not a chance. It'll be graminivorous, a grass eater. Look, the father may have died ten thousand years ago, but the DNA shows that its structure is almost exactly like a modern horse."

Brannigan smiled. "A horse is a horse."

"Of course. The ultrasound scans –"

"Which cost me a fortune," Brannigan interrupted.

"Whatever they cost, the ultrasound scans show a perfectly normal foal. To be precise, it's a colt. A little under the average weight, true, but that's no cause for concern."

Brannigan wasn't really in the mood for talking about the technicalities. "You think the new girl will work out?"

Feyerman shrugged. "Probably. You should keep her here as long as possible after the colt is born. If the mare sees that the girl can accept the colt, perhaps she will too."

"You think there's a possibility that Misty might reject it?"

"It's likely. She knows that something is different."

"But you just said that it's a perfectly normal horse."

"It is, from its appearance. But you of all people should know that animals aren't stupid. The mare senses our concern. The more worried we are, the more worried she will be."

"So." Brannigan said. "How soon do we alert the press? I've invested a lot of money in this. I want the maximum amount of publicity. If I can sell three or four colts or fillies on the publicity, I'll make my money back even if the foal is stillborn."

Feyerman smiled. "Well, that is a relief. For a moment I thought you were actually concerned for the horse's well-being."

Brannigan laughed. "Only as far as the money goes."

"Of course, you still owe me half a million pounds. I expect to get it as soon as the colt is born, alive or dead."

"And I thought you were doing this for the good of science," Brannigan said, his voice heavy with sarcasm.

Feyerman smiled again. "Like you, I'm only doing this for the money."

CHAPTER III

Cathy returned home that night, and when she told her aunt that she had a fulltime job with full board for the summer, Margaret's attitude changed immediately.

In the back of her mind, Cathy had thought that Margaret would suddenly become protective, afraid that something might happen. But Margaret was delighted with the news. She helped Cathy pack, gave her some money to keep her going until her first pay cheque, and was in a great mood.

Cathy wasn't sure if Margaret was so happy because of the job, or because she'd have the flat to herself for the next couple of months.

ψ   ψ   ψ

The following day, Damian was waiting for Cathy at the gates. He rushed up to her, and grabbed her by the arm. "Come on! I thought you'd never get here!" He dragged her towards Misty's shed.

"What's the matter?" Cathy asked, running to keep up.

"It's Misty. She's been groaning and crying all night.

She won't eat and won't let anyone near her. I think she's missing you!"

They arrived at the shed, and Cathy ran inside to see Misty lying on the ground. She dropped her bag and knelt down beside the horse. "Misty? Are you okay?"

The horse raised her head slightly, and looked at Cathy.

Damian stood in the doorway. "She's been like that since you left last night. Brannigan was going mad!"

Cathy rubbed her hand along Misty's neck. "She's very hot. Damian, can you bring some water?"

He nodded and ran out, returning with a steel bucket. Water sloshed onto the floor as he placed it in front of Misty.

Cathy tested the water. "It's warm."

"It's supposed to be. If she drinks cold water when she has a fever she could get cramps."

"Does she have enough food?" Cathy asked.

Damian nodded. "Yes, but she hasn't touched it."

Misty looked at Cathy, then at Damian.

"Can you leave us for a few minutes?" Cathy asked. "I'll try and get her to eat."

Once he had left, Misty reached her head into the bucket and began to drink. Cathy continued stroking her. "Poor Misty," she said. "You don't know what's happening to you."

She looked at the horse's swollen belly. In the half-light, Cathy thought she could see the foal moving slightly, but she wasn't sure if it was just the way the horse was breathing.

By the end of the day, Cathy was exhausted. She'd managed to get Misty to eat, then she cleaned the shed again and spent the afternoon with the horse, gently chatting to her and grooming her coat the way Damian had shown her. Cathy plaited Misty's mane and tail, and by the time Damian returned at six, Misty was transformed.

Damian grinned. "All right. What have you done with the other horse? This can't be the same animal I left you with this morning."

"She's in much better form now," Cathy said. "All the dirt and grime has transferred to me."

"Come on. I'll show you to the guest rooms."

"Rooms? You mean there's more than one?"

Damian laughed. "The people who stay in the guest rooms are usually rich enough to buy this whole farm a hundred times over!"

When she saw the rooms, Cathy could well believe it. The guest suite was an apartment bigger than her Aunt Margaret's flat. The walls had been painted a dazzling white, and huge framed paintings and photos of horses hung in all the rooms.

There was a huge bedroom, complete with a stereo, TV and video, a bathroom with a bath big enough to swim in, and a kitchen-cum-sittingroom with enough equipment to open a shop.

It looked like it had never been used, Cathy pointed out to Damian.

"We don't often have guests, but when we do they tend to arrive out of the blue. Everything has to be ready." He checked his watch. "Right. You're probably starving. If you're ready in half an hour you can have dinner with me and the wife."

When Damian left, Cathy unpacked her things as quickly as possible, and had the fastest shower of her life.

She ran back out to Misty's shed and looked in. The horse was peacefully asleep.

Cathy left the shed just in time to see Damian driving up in a large Land Rover. He waved her over, and she climbed into the passenger seat. Cathy knew less about cars than she did about horses, and asked Damian about it.

"To be honest, I don't know much about these things, except how to drive them. Brannigan – I mean *Mister* Brannigan – gave me this last year. I taught myself how to drive."

From the way he seemed to hit every pot-hole in the road, Cathy had guessed that for herself.

ψ   ψ   ψ

Annette, Damian's wife, seemed delighted to have a guest for dinner. While Damian was in the kitchen swearing over the cooking, she brought Cathy on a tour of the house. Cathy found herself telling Annette all about her aunt, and how she came to be living with her.

"And you're really not happy there?" Annette said.

"I hate it. That's why I jumped at the chance of looking

after Misty. Now I won't be spending the entire summer locked up in the house."

"Don't you miss your friends from Waterford?"

"Sort of. But I was never really very close to them. I mean, none of them has ever written to me. That shows how much they miss me."

Annette smiled. "Ah, but have you written to them?"

"Sure I have! Loads of times!" She paused. "Well, once or twice," she added.

"Well, don't worry about them. A lot of people only meet one or two special friends in their lives. You probably just haven't met yours yet."

"And have you?"

The older woman smiled again. "I married him. It's funny, but Damian can be selfish, and childish, and bad-tempered, and moody, but he's still just about the most wonderful person I've ever met. You know what I think, Cathy? They say that a good friend is someone who will always stand up for you when you're in the right. Well, I disagree with that. Almost anyone will stand up for you when you're in the right. A good friend is someone who will stand up for you when you're in the wrong."

Cathy laughed. "That's a nice way of looking at it!"

From the kitchen there came the sound of a plate smashing off the floor, followed by a muttered string of swear words.

Annette closed her eyes and shook her head in bemusement. "I don't want to know."

ψ   ψ   ψ

Later, Damian drove Cathy back to the farm. When they reached the main gate, Damian got out and opened the passenger door. "Move over," he said.

Cathy stared at him. "What?"

"Move over. Into the driver's seat. You want to learn to drive, don't you?"

"Do I?"

"Of course you do!" Damian said. "Everyone wants to learn how to drive."

"Well, yes, of course. I mean, eventually. But not *yet!*"

"Why not?"

"I'm far too young to drive! It's illegal!"

He shook his head. "No it's not. Not on private land. Go on, move over."

After an hour Cathy was a shivering wreck. They had driven about a hundred metres in total, and had bumped into three walls and driven over a bucket.

Damian laughed at her nervousness. "Don't worry, you'll get used to it. Just remember to ease off the clutch *gently*, don't just pull your foot up. Anyway, I'd better get back. I'd advise you to get some sleep. We start at six in the morning."

"Six! You're kidding!"

He grinned. "Nope. Six. You'll be ready?"

Cathy sighed, and nodded. "I'll be ready."

She paid a last visit to Misty before she went back to the guest suite. The horse was sleeping deeply, her breathing was rough and she seemed to be cold. Cathy took a blanket from a hook on the wall and draped it over the horse.

ψ   ψ   ψ

Dr Emil Feyerman tapped away at his computer. The lights were off in his office, the only illumination coming from the screen.

He was worried about the unborn colt. He hadn't told Brannigan, but something was very wrong.

The DNA structures of the frozen horse had been fairly normal, and he hadn't had much difficulty encoding Misty's egg with the missing chromosomes. It was Misty herself that worried him.

A birth is a traumatic thing for any animal, especially a horse, with such a long gestation period, and he'd seen horses reject their offspring because they were different in some way. And this colt would be so very different: its parents separated by ten thousand years.

Even more worrying was the possibility that the colt might be stillborn, or might die in the birth process if Misty was in great enough pain. He didn't want to risk any strong pain-killers, so Misty would certainly be suffering.

And of course if the horse was upset, she might deliver early, thus greatly increasing the risk to the colt.

ψ   ψ   ψ

Misty went into labour two weeks early. Both Roger Brannigan and Emil Feyerman were out of the country and couldn't be contacted.

Damian phoned the vet as soon as he realised what was happening, but Misty – even though she was suffering greatly – wouldn't let anyone but Cathy near her.

The vet was a tall country woman. She was well-dressed and looked as though she'd been preparing for a night out. She didn't seem to mind having to cancel her date, but she was extremely annoyed that Misty wouldn't let her approach. The horse panicked whenever Damian or the vet came any closer than the door, and the vet knew that if Misty was panicking, the birth would be that much harder.

Cathy sat by the horse while Damian and the vet looked on from the doorway. It was almost ten at night, and the light was fading fast. There were no electric lights in the shed, but Damian had brought a couple of kerosene lamps and a torch.

The vet spoke softly to Cathy. "If she doesn't let us near her, Cathy, you'll have to help, okay?"

Cathy swallowed. "Help? What, you mean help with the delivery?"

The older woman nodded. "Don't worry. Birth is a natural process. I'll tell you what to do."

As the hours passed, Misty began to bellow in pain. Cathy held on and tried to soothe the horse, but she wasn't sure how much good she was doing.

And then it happened, Misty's bellows grew much

stronger, her body was quivering and bucking in spasms. The vet shouted at Cathy to get behind the horse.

With Misty blocking most of the light, Cathy could barely see anything. She felt something wet on Misty's legs, and she guessed it was the placenta. She could feel the colt as it emerged from the womb, and it seemed so small. It dropped gently to the ground as Misty gave one final, shuddering cry.

Then the moon broke though the clouds and shone through the shed's skylight. Standing before Cathy, covered in fluids and small traces of blood, was a perfect white foal.

CHAPTER IV

Misty died half an hour after her foal was born. Cathy cried as she led the colt to a specially prepared stable, but she did her best not to let the colt see how upset she was. She knew that he would be able to sense her emotions.

If Cathy had known more about horses, or had seen a baby foal before, she might have noticed that this one was different.

Damian noticed it, but said nothing to Cathy. When she had left, he talked to the vet.

"That is one strong little horse, Doc."

She nodded. "I know. It looks like it's already a couple of days old. What's going on here?"

Damian looked guilty. "I don't know what you mean," he lied.

"Mr Brannigan offered me a lot of money to be on call for the birth. He seemed very uptight about it. He mentioned a Dr Feyerman."

"Emil Feyerman. He's a genetic scientist. He was looking after Misty."

"Why?"

Damian did his best to look innocent. "I'm not sure." He paused. "All right, I am sure. But I was sworn to secrecy."

The vet glared at him. "Was there anything you could have told me that would have saved the mare?"

"Nothing. I don't think they were expecting anything like this."

"And what *were* they expecting?"

He shook his head. "Sorry. I can't tell you."

ψ   ψ   ψ

The small stable had been scrubbed perfectly clean and was insulated from the cold night air. There was a bright fluorescent light in the ceiling, and Cathy saw that its brightness could be adjusted. She turned it down, not wanting to blind the horse. There was a basin of warm water and a set of sponges and towels waiting, and Cathy realised with annoyance that the stable had been prepared a long time ago, almost as if they were expecting Misty to die.

The little colt settled down on a bed of fresh straw, and gazed up at Cathy. She smiled at him, brushing away the last of her tears. "All right, so your mammy's gone, but I'm here to look after you now. I'll do my best."

She soaked a sponge and began to clean the foal. It nuzzled against her, and tried to nibble her hair.

When the colt was clean, Cathy had her first good look at it. He seemed a bit on the small side, but then she wasn't sure about that. Also, he was pure white, where his mother was a solid dark brown. Cathy wondered who the father was.

Damian and the vet arrived shortly. The vet knelt down and examined the colt, then proclaimed him to be in perfect health. Cathy couldn't help noticing the glances between the vet and Damian.

"What's wrong?"

"Nothing," Damian said. "Why?"

"You seem to be a bit nervous," Cathy said.

He laughed softly. "Not at all. I'm just knackered."

The vet got up to leave. "Someone should stay with him tonight. I'll be back first thing in the morning, but call me if there are any problems."

After she'd left, Damian turned back to Cathy. "So, what are you going to call him?"

"Me? Do I get to name him?"

He nodded. "Yep. After all, you were there. Besides, you're his mammy now."

Cathy sighed. "Don't say that. What's he going to do without a mother?"

"Now don't worry. This isn't the first time something like this has happened, you know. You'll have to feed him from a bottle and keep him clean until he can look after himself."

"How soon will that be?"

"With this guy, who can tell? A couple of weeks, probably. Feyerman will know better."

"Feyerman!" Cathy said in disgust. "I don't like him much."

"Neither do I, but he was responsible for this little fella here."

Cathy was intrigued. "How come?"

"It's a long story."

She looked around, then indicated the colt. "We've got plenty of time."

Damian told Cathy the story of the prehistoric horse, and how Feyerman and Brannigan had decided to try and re-create it. He looked at the sleeping colt as he finished. "It appears to have been a success. So, what are you going to call him?"

"I don't know. I mean, what sort of names do you usually give horses?"

"It's up to you. Whatever you think."

Cathy thought back to when, just a few hours earlier, she had first seen the colt, alive and glistening in the moonlight.

She smiled. "His name is Moonlight."

ψ   ψ   ψ

Roger Brannigan and Dr Emil Feyerman arrived three days later. They went straight to Moonlight's stable, to find Cathy feeding him from a bottle.

"How is he?" Brannigan asked.

Cathy smiled. "He's fine! He's been eating like, well, like a horse!"

Feyerman nodded. "Good." He knelt down in front of the colt. "Strange, though. He's growing fast. *Very* fast."

"Is that dangerous?" Cathy asked.

The scientist ignored her, and turned to Brannigan. "I want to run a complete check on it. Blood and tissue samples, mass to volume ratio, ultrasound scans. Everything." He smiled to himself, and absently began to stroke Moonlight's mane.

"A pure white colt. He's a beauty, all right. How steady is he on his feet?" Brannigan asked.

Cathy stood up, and put the bottle aside. "Come on, Moonlight! Up!"

The colt pushed himself to his feet, and gazed quizzically up at the others.

"Well," Feyerman said, "At least he doesn't have his mother's animosity."

"He's very friendly," Cathy said.

"Good. Bring him out. The north field, I think."

Cathy followed the men outside, the colt trotting lightly after her. She noticed that, as they walked, Moonlight tried to keep her between himself and the two men. He's a good judge of character, she thought.

The field was quite small, less than three acres, but it must have seemed huge to Moonlight. As soon as Cathy let go of him, he bounded forward. Laughing, Cathy ran after him.

Roger Brannigan turned to Feyerman. "I owe you half a million pounds," he said with a smile.

"This is true. You know, I'm rather pleased with myself. That little horse is something special."

"You seemed worried about his accelerated growth."

The scientist shrugged. "It could be nothing, but I've a

39

feeling that he'll reach maturity very quickly."

"This is getting better and better!" Brannigan said. "Faster growth means greater profits! Did you plan for this?"

Feyerman shook his head. "No. It must be inherent to that particular strain of *Equus Caballus*. I wonder ... You realise of course that faster growth generally means a shorter lifespan, don't you?"

Brannigan nodded. "True. However, this is no ordinary animal. Maybe he's inherited his father's growth but his mother's longevity."

Feyerman raised an eyebrow in disbelief. "Let's not speculate until we see the results."

They left Cathy and Moonlight playing in the field, and walked back to Brannigan's office.

"Did you notice the colt's skull?" Feyerman asked as they walked.

"It did seem a little out of shape. A birth defect, perhaps?"

"I won't be able to tell until we get the results of the tests."

ψ   ψ   ψ

Cathy stayed with Moonlight while Dr Feyerman took the blood and tissue samples from the colt. She had been worried that it might in some way hurt him, but the scientist took only tiny skin scrapings and a few drops of blood.

When he'd finished, Feyerman examined Moonlight's

head. He turned it from side to side, fascinated with the way Moonlight refused to take his eyes off him. Feyerman ran his hand over Moonlight's forehead, where, just above the eyes, he thought he could feel a slight bump.

Feyerman left, and Cathy sat on the ground beside Moonlight, hugging the colt as he watched the scientist make his way across the courtyard. She could feel how Moonlight's neck muscles were tensed up. Cathy sighed.

ψ   ψ   ψ

"At first I thought it was a defect in the skull," Feyerman said. "But it turned out to be just a clump of matted hair."

"That's a relief," Brannigan said. "I was a bit worried about that."

It was late in the evening, and the two men were sitting in Brannigan's study, going over the results of the test.

"There's something you should know," Feyerman said. "This is no ordinary horse."

"I should hope not. It cost enough."

"Forget the cost for the moment. In fact, don't even alert the press until I give the word."

Brannigan frowned. "What's the matter?"

"I've given the colt every examination I can think of, and I can't understand how it's growing so fast. Its blood cells were so alive you wouldn't believe it. And the tissue samples ... Something just doesn't add up. The horse is getting energy out of nothing. You saw how fast it was. I'll bet it's bloody strong too."

"Why is that a problem?"

"Let's look at the facts, eh? We've reconstructed a genus of horse that probably died out over ten thousand years ago. It's bounding with energy that it shouldn't have, and growing at a startling speed. And the matted hair on its forehead ... "

"You keep coming back to that! What's the significance?"

The scientist leaned back in his chair. "Have you ever seen the way a cow's horns are cut off? They use a saw. An ordinary woodsaw, usually, and there's no pain. The horns aren't made of bone. It's just hair. Matted hair."

Brannigan was silent for a long time. He stood and walked to the window, looking out into the darkness.

Feyerman spoke. "There *are* legends about this."

The other man nodded. "I know. But legends are ... No. This is not possible."

"It's not only possible, Roger, it's true. Give him a couple of weeks, you'll see. The clump of matted hair will grow."

"Into a horn," Brannigan said, his voice barely a whisper.

Feyerman nodded. "A horn. The legends are true, you see. A pure white horse, with a single horn." He gave a short laugh. "We've done more than given life to a prehistoric horse, Roger! We've given life to a unicorn!"

CHAPTER V

Over the next few weeks, Cathy and Moonlight played constantly in the fields. Not being used to horses, Cathy didn't notice anything unusual about the speed at which the colt was growing, and no-one volunteered the information.

The other workers on the stud farm had been instructed to stay away from Cathy and Moonlight, and only Roger Brannigan, Emil Feyerman and Damian Corscadden were allowed near the unicorn.

Brannigan and Feyerman kept the animal's secret to themselves, afraid of what might happen if the press were to get wind of the story before they were certain that Moonlight would live. Feyerman had decided that the colt should be watched closely for a few months, until they were certain that it was normal in all other respects, before announcing it to the world.

When Moonlight was six weeks old, Cathy noticed that the bump on his forehead was beginning to show. Previously, she could tell it was there only by touch, but now it was quite prominent. She asked Damian about it, but the young man was forced to admit that he was puzzled.

"I've never seen anything like this before, Cathy, but I'm sure it's all right. I mean, Feyerman would have said something. He does know that the bump is there, doesn't he?"

"He certainly does. That's the first thing he checks every morning."

"And how does he seem about it? I mean, does he look worried?"

Cathy shook her head. "No, not at all. In fact, he always smiles."

"I told you about the frozen horse they found in that glacier, didn't I?"

"The horse that was Moonlight's daddy. I remember seeing it on the news last year."

"Then you'll remember that the horse's head was missing, right? I wonder if there's a connection?"

Cathy stroked Moonlight's neck, and smiled at the colt. "Don't worry, Moonlight! No-one's going to harm you!"

Damian laughed. "He can't understand you, you know."

"Of course he can! Can't you, Moonlight?"

The colt gave a snort.

"See?" Cathy said. "He said 'Yes'!"

"All right, Moonlight. What do you get if you multiply six by nine?"

Moonlight tilted his head towards Cathy, then snorted again.

"How do you expect him to answer?" Cathy said. "He can't speak, you know!"

Damian laughed again. "But he *can* understand!"

"He can!" Cathy said indignantly. "Moonlight, prove it. Get up and walk around Damian in a circle."

Moonlight gave Cathy a look as if to say "Do I have to?", but he got to his feet, walked around Damian once and stood looking at him. He let out another snort.

Damian didn't know how to react. He sat unmoving, staring at the ground, for a few moments. Then he looked at Cathy. "Whatever you do, don't mention this to Feyerman or Brannigan, all right?"

"Why not? What would they do?"

"I don't know. And I don't want to find out. Just don't say a word, okay?"

"Okay."

Damian got to his feet and walked towards the door. He looked back and smiled. "You were right. Moonlight, from now on just pretend to be a normal, ordinary horse, okay?"

Moonlight lowered his head slightly, then raised it again.

My God, Damian said to himself, he's trying to nod!

ψ   ψ   ψ

"We'll have to take him away from here," Feyerman told Brannigan. "The workers are becoming too suspicious."

"I know. But what can we do?"

"You have another house in Wicklow, don't you? It has a stable."

"Well, yes. But no-one's staying there at the moment.

Who'll look after Moonlight?"

"I will. I can set up my laboratory there. We need a few more months before the unicorn becomes public knowledge, and to be honest I don't trust anyone else to keep it a secret."

"It could be difficult," Brannigan said. "He's very attached to Cathy."

"He'll just have to become unattached. Look, when you get right down to it, he's just another horse, right? Mutated, perhaps, but not in any other way out of the ordinary."

"I don't know about that. The way he's growing, his energy. There's something very different about that."

"Even so, that's all the more reason why we should take him away."

Brannigan nodded. "Okay. You're right. But when?"

"The sooner the better. What about tomorrow morning?"

ψ   ψ   ψ

Cathy was usually up and out of bed by half-five in the morning, and the first to see Moonlight, so it was with a shock that she realised that Brannigan and Feyerman were already in with him.

Cathy also saw, to her horror, that there was a truck with a horsebox waiting in the courtyard.

She rushed into the stable. "Don't do it! Don't take him away!"

Brannigan turned to her. "Cathy. Look, it's for his own

good. You know that Moonlight's not ... Normal. He needs special attention, and only Dr Feyerman can give it to him."

She glared at the scientist. "There's nothing wrong with him!"

Feyerman gave her a weak smile. "I'm sorry, Cathy, but Moonlight's not well. We have to take him to somewhere safer."

"Where?"

The scientist started to answer, then raised his eyes in disgust and turned to Brannigan. "You deal with her. She's your problem."

Brannigan led Cathy outside. "Cathy, we know what we're doing. Trust us."

"But what about me? He needs me!"

"No he doesn't. He's just another horse. There are plenty more like him on the farm. You can look after one of the other ones."

"I don't want one of the other ones! I want Moonlight!" Cathy realised that she was becoming hysterical, but she wasn't going to give up without a fight.

"Look at it this way. Moonlight is *my* horse, okay? What I say goes. Now either you forget about him or you pack your bags and go home. Which is it to be?"

Cathy took a deep breath. "Can't I go with him?"

"No."

"Then I'm leaving," she said. "Today."

"If that's the way you want it. I'll have the secretary give you your cheque."

"Keep your stupid money!" Cathy shouted. "That's all you think about! Money! You think that's why I'm here? Not everyone in the world is obsessed with money, you know."

Brannigan glared at her. "That's enough! Now get your things and get out of here!"

Cathy stormed off, tears flowing down her cheeks. She packed her bag as quickly as she could, then left the guest suite.

As she entered the courtyard, she saw Feyerman leading Moonlight into the horsebox. Moonlight saw Cathy and tried to run towards her, but Feyerman pulled back on the rope he'd tied around the horse's neck.

Moonlight was forced into the horsebox, and the ramp was slammed into place and locked.

Cathy turned away and walked towards the main road. As she walked, the truck drove past her. She could see Moonlight inside, looking out, his eyes pleading with her.

She ran, but the truck was going too fast. Cathy was out of breath as it turned the corner, and drove out into the early morning traffic.

ψ   ψ   ψ

It was almost eleven by the time Cathy got back to the flat. She'd been afraid to hitch a lift, and had walked almost five miles before she saw a bus going in the right direction.

She was surprised to find her Aunt Margaret at home. It was a Wednesday, and she should have been in work.

Margaret looked startled. "What happened? I thought you weren't due home for another month!"

Cathy dropped her bag and began to cry. She buried her face in her hands, sobbing, hoping that Margaret would come over and hug her, tell her everything was all right.

But Margaret simply ignored her, and continued watching the television.

Cathy had never felt so alone in her life.

CHAPTER VI

Cathy spent the next month preparing for school, trying to take her mind off Moonlight. Margaret was at home most of the day. She'd started going out with a wealthy older man, and had given up her job. Cathy thought she was a fool, but didn't say anything.

Stephen Harrington, Margaret's boyfriend, was in his late forties, and he tended to arrive at odd hours. Cathy suspected that he was married, but as nothing was ever said about his home life or his job, she wasn't quite sure.

Margaret did seem a lot happier now. She had lots of free time, and Stephen paid the rent on the flat and was always buying presents for her. He didn't seem to mind Cathy around the flat – it gave him an extra chance to show off.

He was always dressed impeccably, with suits from Philip's of London and Christian Dior glasses. Sometimes he brought presents for Cathy, usually stuffed animals or sweets, though once he gave her a Swiss Army knife. He was always polite and charming, and he had an answer to every problem.

Cathy couldn't stand him. *Nobody* is that nice, she

reasoned. He *must* be married or something. All the presents are just to prove how nice he is. If he was really nice, he wouldn't need to give us presents.

The day after Cathy returned to school, Stephen came back from a business trip to Florida. He brought Margaret a set of diamond earrings with a matching necklace, and for Cathy a fluffy toy unicorn.

That was when Cathy's dreams started.

The first night, she dreamt that Moonlight had grown, and the bump on his forehead had turned into a golden twisted horn. His mane and tail had changed colour, a sort of whitish gold.

And in her dream she saw Moonlight racing across the open country, hunted by a man on a vicious black stallion. She couldn't quite see the man's face, and when she tried to concentrate on his features, she woke up.

It was half-past six in the morning, and Cathy knew that she wouldn't be able to get back to sleep, so she washed and dressed, and prepared for school.

It was a long day. Cathy couldn't believe how each class dragged. When they were finally released, she ran home and picked up the phone.

She called Lowlands, and asked to speak to Damian. When he finally got to the phone, Cathy asked him about Moonlight.

"I haven't heard anything," Damian said. "Feyerman hasn't been around since he took Moonlight away. How are *you*, anyway? You left us without a word."

"I'm okay," Cathy said. "I just miss him."

"I'm sure they know what they're doing, Cathy. They won't harm him."

Cathy sighed. "I had a dream about Moonlight last night. There was someone chasing him."

Damian laughed gently. "It's just a dream. I'm sure he's all right."

They spoke for a while longer. Cathy wondered whether to tell Damian that in the dream Moonlight had been a unicorn, but she decided against it. Damian reminded Cathy that she still hadn't been paid, and he promised to send on the cheque.

Cathy felt different when she put down the phone. She decided that Moonlight had probably forgotten all about her, and she'd be best to do the same.

ψ   ψ   ψ

Just over a week later, Cathy had another dream about Moonlight. In this one, she was riding on his back as he thundered along a sandy beach.

The dream felt good, and right. There was no danger.

They stopped for a short while. Moonlight chomped at some of the scrub grass growing on a dune, while Cathy sat watching him.

"How are you today?" she asked.

Moonlight lifted his head towards her, and in her mind she heard a voice.

I'm fine. It's been too long since I had a run along the beach.

"You look good," Cathy said. "The open air suits you. Your coat's getting a very healthy sheen."

Moonlight walked over, and nudged his head against hers. *Thank you for rescuing me. You saved my life.*

Suddenly Cathy was confused. She couldn't remember rescuing Moonlight. Then, as she tried to think about it, she slowly began to realise that this was a dream. She woke up, clutching her pillow and crying softly.

ψ   ψ   ψ

As the weeks wore on, Cathy began to have the dreams almost every night.

Once she dreamt that she was back on the farm, the morning that they were taking Moonlight away. But in the dream, as she argued with Brannigan, Moonlight kicked out at Dr Feyerman as he tried to tie the rope around his neck.

Moonlight darted from the stable, heading for the fields. Cathy ran after him, leaving the two men far behind.

Though Moonlight was going at full speed, Cathy found it easy to keep up with him. They ran side by side, happy to be together and free.

They stopped beside a small stream. Cathy dropped to her knees, exhausted, but Moonlight wasn't even out of breath.

"It's magic, isn't it?" Cathy asked.

Moonlight nodded.

"And this is another dream?"

He nodded again.

As she watched, Moonlight began to grow. The bump

on his head became a horn, and his frame widened. He was the size of an adult donkey, then a pony, and still growing. When he stopped, Cathy stood up and walked over to him. She was shivering slightly, unsure of what to do.

Don't be afraid, Cathy.

Then the scene changed, and Moonlight was lying on his side in the middle of a darkened laboratory, connected to feeding tubes and a catheter. There was a bundle of wires leading from his head to what looked like an expensive computer.

"What is this place?" Cathy asked.

This is where I am now, in the real world. His eyes pleaded with her. *There is so much pain, Cathy. Take me away from here!*

"But how? Where are you?"

Then she woke. It was another schoolday. She sat up in bed for almost an hour, wondering what to do.

By the time she reached school, Cathy had decided that she would rescue Moonlight, no matter what it took.

Ψ   Ψ   Ψ

The next night, Moonlight didn't appear in her dream at first. Cathy found herself outside a large house. From the sounds and smells she was somewhere in the country. The door was open, and she walked in. There was no-one around, and it seemed that there hadn't been anyone there for some time. There was a small pile of unopened letters lying inside the door, and a fine coat of dust almost everywhere.

She found herself compelled to explore the house, and discovered handprints in the dust on the banisters. She walked up, and saw that one of the bedrooms was in use.

There were clothes dumped in one corner, and a stack of handwritten notes on the dressing table. She recognised the handwriting as Dr Emil Feyerman's.

She went downstairs again, and found that the kitchen was in a mess. Dirty plates and cups were everywhere, and newspapers were strewn about the kitchen table. A door opened onto the huge back garden, and Cathy went out.

There was a single large stable at the top of the garden, its door bolted and padlocked. Through a knot-hole she could see Moonlight. It was the same place as in last night's dream.

She gasped in shock, and suddenly found herself standing just inside the front door.

Cathy couldn't understand this dream. How could this help her to rescue Moonlight? All right, she knew what the place looked like, where he was being kept, but exactly where was she?

Then Cathy looked down at the pile of letters. She picked one up and read the address. She smiled to herself. "Hold on, Moonlight. I'm coming!"

CHAPTER VII

When Cathy woke the address was firmly planted in her mind: "Roger Brannigan, Furlongs, Dunlavin, County Wicklow", but she knew that it wasn't going to be as simple as getting on a bus.

It was Friday. Cathy made her lunch and went off to school as usual. She spent the day gazing out of the window, much to the annoyance of her teachers, then deliberately delayed on the way home.

Margaret was in her usual position in front of the TV when Cathy got back to the flat. Cathy pretended to be excited, and told Margaret that one of the girls in school had asked her if she wanted to stay for the weekend.

Her aunt just grunted, and continued watching the television.

"So can I go, then?" Cathy asked.

"Yeah, sure. When?"

"Tonight! I'm to meet Julie at half-five outside the bookshop, or inside if it's raining."

Margaret brightened up. "Tonight? Well, of course you can go! When will you be back?"

"Sunday night, probably. Though I might stay over and

just go straight into school on Monday morning."

"Well, you'd better get ready!"

Cathy went into her room, and as she walked she could hear Margaret picking up the phone. She's probably phoning Stephen to tell him that they'll have an empty flat for the weekend, Cathy thought.

She looked around her bedroom, trying to decide what to bring. Clothes and money, obviously, but what else? She picked up the Swiss Army knife that Stephen had given her, and tucked it into the pocket of her jeans. She grabbed her bag and stuffed it with clothes, and changed into her runners.

Then she went into the kitchen and began to make sandwiches. Cathy had no idea how long she'd be away, or even if she was ever going to come back, so she thought that it might be wise to stock up.

She used almost one whole large sliced pan, making triple-decker sandwiches with tomatoes and cheese, and a few with banana and peanut butter, which was her favourite. She took half a dozen apples from the basket, and put them in with the sandwiches.

Cathy had already lodged the cheque that Damian had sent, and it came to just over five hundred pounds. She had two hundred of that in cash, and she knew that she could get the rest from the Banklink machine when she needed it. On an impulse, she took the toy unicorn that Stephen had brought her back from Florida, and put it in her bag.

When Cathy left the kitchen, Margaret noticed the bag

of food. "Where are you going with all *that?*"

Cathy paused. "Em ... Well, you see Julie's parents aren't going to be there, so we decided we'd need to bring food."

"I see. So Julie doesn't have any food of her own, then?"

"Well, since I'm going to be her guest I thought that it'd only be polite to bring something."

Margaret seemed satisfied with the answer, and left it at that.

"That was close," Cathy said to herself as she shut her bedroom door. She sat on the bed and went over everything again. On an impulse she packed her torch and her Walkman. After all, she might have to walk around in the dark, and would certainly be spending a lot of time on the bus. Wearing a Walkman was one sure way to prevent people from asking you where you were going.

ψ   ψ   ψ

At five o'clock, Cathy picked up her bag and left her room. She said goodbye to Margaret, and left the flat.

Suddenly, Cathy realised that she hadn't the faintest idea of how to get to Dunlavin. She didn't even know where it was.

First things first, she said to herself. Get a train to Bray, that's in County Wicklow. After that there must be a bus or something.

She walked into the city centre, then along the quays until she reached Tara Street station. Rush hour on a Friday is not the time to see the station at its best, and

Cathy spent a terrifying ten minutes in the ticket queue, afraid that someone would look at her and guess that she was running away from home.

Running away from home. She hadn't thought of it like that, but that's what it was. What will happen when Monday night comes and I'm not home? she wondered. Will Margaret phone the police? Will she even notice that I'm missing? And then, when the police discover that Margaret doesn't know where I'm supposed to be staying, she'll be in a lot of trouble.

Cathy felt guilty for a few minutes, but then she decided that if Margaret didn't care enough to *ask* where she would be staying, then she could just suffer the consequences.

The DART, when it finally arrived, was packed. Cathy was forced to stand, and only got a seat when most of the people got off at Dun Laoghaire.

She arrived in Bray just before seven o'clock, and stood outside the station wondering where to go. A young woman pushing a buggy – who got onto the train at Sandycove – noticed Cathy's look of confusion and came over.

"Are you lost?" The woman had short blond hair and kind blue eyes, and was about twenty-five. The baby boy in the buggy was obviously her son. He had the same blue eyes and blond hair, and he giggled mischievously at Cathy.

Cathy smiled. "I'm sort of lost. I'm trying to get to Dunlavin."

The young woman shook her head. "I've never heard of it. Is it somewhere *in* Bray?"

"No. I mean, I don't think so."

"You're running away from home, aren't you?"

Cathy blushed. She thought about lying, but the woman didn't seem the sort who was going to turn her in to the police. "Well, I'm giving it a go."

"We've got an hour to wait for our bus to Kilpedder. Haven't we, Shane?"

The boy looked up and giggled again.

Shane's mother smiled at Cathy. "Let's go and have something to eat. You can tell me all about it."

ψ   ψ   ψ

They went to a small, rather grotty café, and ordered fish and chips. The young woman, whose name was Sheelagh, waited until Cathy had finished telling her story before she spoke.

"And you're running away from home just to be with a *horse?*" Sheelagh asked.

Cathy had left out the details of Moonlight's creation, and the dreams in which he was a unicorn. "I know it sounds silly, but –"

"It's okay. I've heard worse reasons. But will finding Moonlight solve any of your problems?"

Cathy shrugged. "I don't know. It'll probably make a whole new set of problems for me."

"Look, I'll tell you what. You tell me where you're going, okay? Then if you're reported missing I'll phone the police and give them the address, just in case something happens."

"But I might not want to be found."

"In that case," Sheelagh said, writing on a napkin, "here's my phone number. Give me a ring if there's any trouble, or if you don't want to be found, or if you just want someone to talk to, okay?"

Cathy was so relieved to have found a friend that she almost started to cry.

Beside them, sitting up in his buggy, Shane was chewing methodically on a chip that was so big he needed both hands to hold it. There were bits of half-chewed chips littered around the buggy. Sheelagh raised her eyes, and began to pick them up. "I'm going to have to teach him to *eat* his food, not play with it."

Cathy laughed. "He's gorgeous. Is he like his father?"

"Well, sometimes. That's one thing that really annoys me. People keep telling me who they think he's like, but I just say that he's like himself."

Cathy laughed again. "Have you many brothers and sisters?"

"Two sisters, both living in New York, and one brother in Dublin. I'm the only one left at home."

Cathy sighed. "It must be great to have such a normal family."

Sheelagh looked her straight in the eye. "Cathy, there's no such thing as a normal family."

ψ   ψ   ψ

Afterwards, they went into a newsagent's and found a map of County Wicklow. Using that and the bus timetable, they found a private bus that would take Cathy to Naas, just over the border in County Kildare.

"You should try and find somewhere to stay there for tonight," Sheelagh said. "In the morning you'll be able to get to Dunlavin somehow, it's not too far from Naas."

Cathy smiled. "Thanks. You've been very kind." She opened her bag and took out the stuffed toy unicorn. She handed it to Shane. "Here, a present."

Sheelagh smiled. "Ah, now you don't have to."

"I want to. It's the least I can do."

Sheelagh said goodbye and walked away, her son straining out of the buggy for a last smile at Cathy. In his arms he cuddled the toy unicorn.

ψ   ψ   ψ

The bus to Naas was packed with people going home for the weekend, and Cathy almost wasn't allowed on board, but the driver believed her story about how she'd missed the earlier bus.

She had to stand for most of the journey, but eventually the bus began to empty, and she finally got a chance to sit down and rest.

As the bus pulled into Naas, Cathy began to panic again. She still had no idea what to do. She got off and stood at the bus terminus, looking around, then she spotted an old woman struggling home with two large shopping bags. Feeling slightly guilty about what she was going to do, Cathy asked the old woman if she needed any help.

The old woman smiled. "Ah, you're very kind, love. Grab hold of that." She held out a bag for Cathy. "Most young folk wouldn't give you the time of day, let alone offer to help."

Cathy smiled. "It's no problem."

"What's your name, love?"

She paused, wondering whether or not to tell the old woman her name. She decided that it was probably safer to give her real name, because, if anything happened, at least the old woman would remember her. "Cathy. Cathy Donnelly."

"Donnelly, eh? Any relation to the Donnellys who used to live down on Matthew Street?"

"I don't think so."

The old woman then began a long, rambling story detailing the history of the other Donnelly family: which son or daughter had married well, whose children were little brats, the uncle who was an alcoholic but didn't let on, the young one who became pregnant and went off to Manchester for an abortion.

Cathy only half-listened and nodded in what she thought were the right places. Occasionally she said "that's terrible", or "she should have known better", depending on which way the conversation seemed to be leaning.

The woman stopped abruptly. "Well. Here we are. Thanks again, love. You're very kind."

Cathy turned to look at the old woman's house. It was in the middle of a terrace, with a small, well-kept garden and the green and white sign of the Irish Tourist Board outside. She couldn't help smiling.

"Oh! And I was just about to ask you if you knew of any guest houses around here!"

The old woman smiled. "There you go, now. Saint Jude's. The finest guest house in all of Naas, and I should know. But surely you're not thinking of staying here? Aren't you a bit young to be out on your own?"

Cathy shrugged. "I'm seventeen," she lied. "I was supposed to be staying at my cousin's place, but my uncle didn't meet me. He was going to drive up from Dunlavin, but I rang the house and there was no answer."

The old woman's lips had tightened into a straight line, and she frowned heavily. She doesn't believe me, Cathy thought. Her mind raced furiously.

"He's a doctor, you see. Sometimes he gets called out on an emergency. I'll phone later on, my cousins should be in by then."

The old woman relaxed, and pushed open the gate. "Come on in then, love. I'll make you a cup of tea. Sure, if your uncle can't meet you, then you can stay here. At least I'll know you're safe then."

Ψ   Ψ   Ψ

Later that evening, Cathy spent ten minutes speaking to the talking clock, asking it how everything was and when Uncle Billy would be back.

She returned to the kitchen where the old woman, whose name was Mrs O'Neill, was waiting anxiously. "I was right," Cathy said. "There was some emergency. Apparently they were all worried about me. Anyway, I told them I was all right, and I said I'd get the bus over in the morning."

"Ah, well that's okay then," said Mrs O'Neill.

Cathy went to bed at ten o'clock. It was the first time since she left Lowlands that she'd slept in a strange bed, but she was so exhausted that she had no trouble getting to sleep.

She dreamt about Moonlight again. This time there were other unicorns, mostly white but some were golden, with white manes. All were younger than Moonlight. He stood among them proudly. *These will be my children*, Moonlight told her.

The scene changed. Cathy was watching Moonlight fight off the huge black stallion that she'd seen in an earlier dream. Now, she could see a stump on the evil-looking horse's head, where its horn had been cut off.

This was something she hadn't thought of before. Legends told of white and golden unicorns, their lives pure and unselfish. She had never heard of a black unicorn before, but she realised that there was no reason why one should not exist.

The unicorns fought viciously. Moonlight's horn gouged long bloody wounds in the black unicorn's side. The black unicorn screamed, and charged at Moonlight.

Then that scene ended too.

It was morning, and Cathy woke to find the old woman standing over her with a cup of tea. "How are you, dear? All right?"

Cathy smiled. "I'm fine, thanks."

"You've got a busy day ahead of you, you know."

"I know."

Ψ   Ψ   Ψ

It was easy enough to find a coach going to Dunlavin: Cathy called into the tourist office and they told her everything she needed to know.

The coach took nearly an hour to reach Dunlavin, and Cathy spent most of the journey looking out the window and wondering if Moonlight was okay.

At one stage she thought that she must be going mad. She had no evidence that Moonlight was in any danger. And unicorns, especially ones that speak in your mind, just seemed less and less likely the closer she got to Dunlavin.

This is crazy, she said to herself. I'll get to Dunlavin and there'll be nothing there! The house won't even exist. This is all a really, really stupid idea.

Then the driver called out "Dunlavin!"

The bus slowed as it neared the town, and then, just before it stopped, the bus passed a huge, fabulous house. And on the gatepost was a brass plaque bearing the name "Furlongs".

Still in shock, Cathy followed the other passengers off the bus. She walked back to the house, and stood outside the gate, unsure of what to do next.

Then she heard a voice in her mind.

Cathy. I knew you'd come for me!

CHAPTER VIII

There was a time when people accepted magic as part of their everyday lives. It was nothing to be frightened of, it was as normal and as real as the sun rising in the morning.

But things change. Some people began to abuse their abilities to work with magic, and the rest of the people lived in fear.

There was a man, you might call him a wizard, who used his magic to help the crops grow in the nearby fields. No-one ever asked him to, and he never asked payment in return.

The man worked his magic with the help of his friend, an old and wise unicorn. In those times, people and unicorns lived side by side. There were ordinary horses too, of course, but they were as like unicorns as chimpanzees and baboons are like humans.

The unicorn had lived a long time, almost fifty years, and he knew that he was about to die. He and the wizard went to a farmer, and asked that the unicorn be buried in one of the fields he had helped nurture.

The farmer agreed, and soon the unicorn died.

The wizard mourned the passing of his friend, but he knew that the unicorn had lived a full life, and had never brought harm to anyone. Then one day, as the wizard was walking in the field where his friend had been buried, he noticed that the earth around the grave had been freshly turned.

Afraid of what this might mean, he rushed to the farmhouse and demanded to see the farmer. The farmer's son told the wizard that the farmer was busy, but the wizard suspected treachery.

He reached out with his mind, the way the unicorn had taught him, and sensed the farmer in his workshed.

The wizard walked down to the workshed, and without a word, kicked the door open.

Inside he saw the farmer sitting at his bench, a knife in his hand as he cleaned the skull of the unicorn.

In a rage, the wizard began to beat the farmer, but the son pulled him off the cowering man, and demanded to know the meaning of the attack.

The wizard pointed to the unicorn's skull, and said: "He was my friend."

And the farmer said: "He was an animal, nothing more."

"He helped you for years, and this is how you repay his kindness!"

But the farmer and his son would not listen to his pleas, and refused to return the skull to the grave.

The following year, the rains did not come. The sun baked the soil and started fires in the dry, dead cornfields. The well water became stagnant, and soon the farmer and his family were starving.

They went to the wizard for help. "You must stop this! You must end the drought!"

And the wizard said: "I did not cause the drought. For years the unicorn and I prevented it. This year I let it happen. This is all your own doing. Your greed has brought you close to death."

The farmer sobbed, "I am sorry. What can I do?"

And the wizard took them into his own house. He fed them and gave them water. A week later, they returned to their farm to find that it had been utterly destroyed by the heat of the sun.

The farmer blamed the wizard, but his wife held him back. "What's done is done," she said. "It was our own fault. In time we can rebuild our farm. It won't be easy, but that is the price we must pay."

The farmer walked to the ruin of his house, and searched among the rubble until he found the two things for which he was looking. The first was the unicorn's skull. The second was a shovel.

Ψ   Ψ   Ψ

Cathy was sitting on a park bench, enjoying the sunlight and listening to Moonlight's tale. It was almost one in the afternoon, and Moonlight had warned Cathy to stay away from the house until nightfall.

Cathy munched away at her sandwiches as they talked about how things had changed, and Moonlight warned Cathy that – when she saw him – she might not like the way in which he was being kept prisoner.

She answered him in her mind. "I know what it's like. You gave me that dream, remember?"

Of course. But a dream is one thing, reality another.

"How come you can talk to me like this?"

You were there when I was born. You loved me and helped me when I needed someone. You are a good, innocent person,

Cathy. I could have asked for no better.

"How do you know so much? I mean, how can you know what happened in the past, thousands of years ago?"

Memories can be passed on from one generation to the next. We are not like you humans, Cathy. Our power is very strong. We live and die, and live again.

Cathy paused. "I don't know what to do, Moonlight."

Just wait, until tonight. I am very weak here, these machines are draining my power. At night I am strongest.

"Is that because you were born at night?"

All unicorns are born at night. Magic becomes available while the world of men sleeps.

"They say that the moon is magical too, is that true?"

Not in that sense. We see the reflection of the sun's light on the moon, but not only light is reflected. Other forms of energy reach us in the same way, including magic.

"So magic is just a different form of energy? Sorry, Moonlight, but I don't really understand enough about energy. How could magic possibly work?"

If you wind a clock, you use the energy in your muscles to do so. The spring in the clock releases the energy slowly, moving the hands. Muscle energy is turned into machine energy.

"But then what happens? I mean, where does the energy go then? I thought that energy can't be created or destroyed."

The parts of the clock are slowly worn away. This is friction, and the energy turns into heat. Undetectable in such a case, but still heat. The heat from the metal parts warms up the air.

Cathy smiled. "I'm beginning to see what you mean. By winding up a clock I can heat up the room."

Eventually, yes. Another example: plants absorb the energy from the sun, and grow. They die, and are compressed under millions of tons of earth. Then, one day, humanity arrives, and discovers that the carbonised plants have turned into coal. They burn the coal in their power stations ... Solar energy gives electricity, which in turn can give heat and light.

"And where does magic fit into this?"

If a man uses magic to wind a clock, the magic is turned into the potential energy of the spring.

"Where does the man get the magic from in the first place?"

From wherever he gets heat or light, from what he eats. From everything. Magic is the life-force in every living creature. It grows as we grow, building with our experience. It is what shapes us, forms our identities. Magic is what we are.

Ψ   Ψ   Ψ

That evening, as it began to grow dark, Cathy walked back to the house. There was a light in one of the downstairs rooms, and another at the back of the house, Cathy guessed that it was outside the stable where Moonlight was imprisoned.

She waited across the road, half-hidden in the hedges. Moonlight had been growing weaker, and was no longer able to communicate with her. He had done his best to tell her of any problems she might encounter, but he was forced to admit that he would not be able to help her once she began to make her way into the grounds.

It was getting cold, so she zipped up her jacket and slipped her bag onto her back. It was past eleven by the time the lights went off, and another fifteen minutes before she heard the sound of a car starting up.

She kept well back in the hedge while the car pulled out of the driveway, but she was close enough to see that the driver was Dr Emil Feyerman.

She waited another few minutes, her heart beating heavily against her chest.

Okay, she said to herself, go.

Cathy looked around. There was no other traffic on the road, and without streetlights everything was completely dark. Even the moon and stars were hidden behind the thick clouds.

She turned on her torch, keeping the beam on the ground not more than a few feet in front of her, in case anyone was to look in her direction.

The driveway leading up to Furlongs was gravelled. After the first three or four footsteps Cathy realised that there was no way she could walk quietly on the gravel, so she turned onto the grass, aware that she was leaving footprints in the evening dew, but unable to do anything about it.

The driveway led up to the left of the house, ending in a two-car garage. Cathy paused as she reached it, listening carefully.

But there was no sound other than her own anxious breathing.

A gate was set into the wall between the house and the garage. Cathy examined it carefully, standing only a metre away, with the torch held as close to the gate as she could, and, she hoped, her body blocking any reflected light.

The gate was a simple wooden affair, though two metres high, solid and without any handholds. She switched off the torch and looked around again, then, confident that there was no-one around, she stuck the torch in her pocket and jumped for the top of the gate.

Splinters dug themselves into her hands as she pulled herself up, scrabbling with her feet on the wood. She rested for a moment at the top, one leg dangling over each side, then took out her torch again and looked down.

This was something she hadn't anticipated. The ground was much further down on this side, at least three metres. She saw that there were steps leading up to the gate, but Cathy decided she'd rather drop onto the grass even though it was further away: dropping onto the concrete steps was much too dangerous.

She inched her way along the gate and onto the wall, then swung her leg over and dropped heavily to the grass. She slipped in the wet grass as she landed, and felt a sharp pain in her right knee.

Cathy sat on the grass, biting her lip to prevent herself from crying out with the pain. She pushed herself to her feet, and found that she could walk only by holding onto the wall.

She edged her way cautiously around the house, and

with the light of the torch she saw the stable in front of her.

It was securely bolted with a heavy padlock. Swearing to herself, Cathy grabbed the padlock and shook it as hard as she could, hoping that it might come loose, but the door held fast.

She heard a low whinny from inside the stable. "Moonlight? It's me! It's Cathy!"

There was no answer.

ψ　　ψ　　ψ

In an unlocked shed Cathy found a large gardening fork. She jammed the prongs of the fork behind the bolt, and pulled down heavily on the handle.

She could feel the bolt beginning to strain, but even with her full weight the lock didn't break.

She dropped the fork to the ground and stood thinking for a few seconds, then she remembered the Swiss Army knife in her pocket. She opened the screwdriver, and began to remove the screws around the bolt.

It took almost ten minutes, and her hands were cut and blistered by the time the bolt dropped to the ground.

She pulled open the door, shone her torch inside and saw Moonlight.

He was just as he had been in her dream, lying on his side connected to tubes and wires, which in turn were connected to monitoring equipment.

Cathy rushed in, but in the darkness she didn't see the

small white plastic box that was connected to the door frame.

ψ   ψ   ψ

It was another slow night in the local police station, but then it always was.

Garda Connor O'Duffy sat fiddling with his shortwave radio, trying to get the BBC World Service, without any luck. Still, it was Saturday, which meant that his shift on night duty was almost over.

The sergeant was asleep in his office, head down on the desk, using his arm as a pillow.

Saturday nights, while they were always the busiest in any large town, were incredibly dull in Dunlavin.

When the alarm went off O'Duffy dropped his radio in surprise. He heard a muffled shout from the sergeant's office, then both men rushed to the alarm panel and tried to figure out what was going on.

It took them nearly five minutes to find the sheet with the alarm codes, and another two minutes to get through to Naas and let them know what was happening. Then they were in the car, and speeding towards Roger Brannigan's house.

CHAPTER IX

"Moonlight! Are you all right?"

The unicorn was too weak to answer. His legs moved feebly as Cathy entered the darkened stable.

Though she had seen him in her dreams, she couldn't believe how large Moonlight had grown. His horn was solid, twisted and golden, protruding a foot and a half from his forehead, and his mane and tail also had a golden sheen.

She heard a weak voice in her mind.

Cathy ...

"It's okay, Moonlight. I'll get you out of here."

She gently disconnected the feeding tubes and monitoring wires from Moonlight's body. Ignoring the pain in her knee, she knelt down beside him. "Moonlight, can you stand?"

In response, Moonlight twisted his body until his feet were under him, then, clearly with great strain, he managed to push himself to his feet. The first thing he did was knock over a small workbench. Plastic and glass crunched under his feet.

She led the unicorn out of the stable, and realised that

she had no way of getting him off the grounds. "Damn!" She muttered to herself. "I should have thought this out more clearly."

Then a thought struck her. If she could get into the house, she could open the back door and lead Moonlight through.

But how was she going to get in? She could break a window, but then an alarm might go off.

As if in response to this thought, she heard a police siren in the distance. Cathy was smiling to herself at the coincidence when she realised that she might have already tripped an alarm.

She swallowed heavily. The siren was definitely getting closer, and very rapidly.

"Moonlight, we're in trouble."

The unicorn looked around, his ears swivelling as he tried to follow the sounds.

Get on my back, Cathy.

"I can't, Moonlight, I hurt my leg. Anyway, you're too weak!"

He looked at her sternly, then went down on his knees so that Cathy could climb onto his back. The unicorn struggled, but managed to get to his feet once more. He began a slow trot towards the back of the grounds.

Cathy heard the police car stop outside the house, and the voices of the gardai as they began their search.

There was a low farm gate leading to a large field, but Moonlight wasn't strong enough to jump it. He simply crashed through the hedge beside it.

The sound must have been heard by the gardai, because the next thing Cathy knew one of them was shining his powerful torch in their direction.

The gardai shouted and began to run after them.

"Come on, Moonlight! Run!"

I can't, I'm sorry. I'm too weak.

There must be something we can do, Cathy thought. They were half way across the field now, and the younger of the two policemen was gaining on them, shouting at them to stop.

Moonlight picked up speed a little, almost dislodging Cathy from his back.

They neared the end of the field, but it was surrounded by a two-metre-high stone wall. Moonlight kept running, though Cathy could tell that he was getting very weak.

Seeing that they had no escape, the garda slowed down, waiting for them to turn back. The older garda caught up with him, wheezing and red-faced.

Moonlight reached the wall, slowed and stopped.

The gardai approached, still shining their torches into Cathy's face.

"All right, Miss. Take it easy. Where are you going in such a hurry at this time of –"

The moon broke through the clouds, and the gardai got their first look at Moonlight. They stared open-mouthed at the horn on his head.

The younger garda shook his head slowly. "I don't believe it," he said. "I don't believe it."

Cathy looked from one to the other. She patted Moonlight on the neck. "It's okay, Moonlight. It's for the best. At least now Feyerman will stop hurting you."

Moonlight's breathing slowed to normal. He looked at the gardai, and back at the high stone wall. Freedom had been so close.

CHAPTER X

Moonlight looked up at the moon. It had been a long time since he had seen it, and it had never looked so beautiful.

As the gardai came closer, staring at him in amazement, Moonlight began to feel dizzy.

At first, he thought he was about to collapse from the exertion, then he realised what was happening.

Cathy, hold on.

Moonlight tensed his powerful legs, and cleared the wall in a standing jump.

Ψ   Ψ   Ψ

Much later, Cathy and Moonlight were deep in the Wicklow mountains. Moonlight had found a fallen tree in the forest, and he and Cathy lay down beside it and slept for the night.

Neither of them had ever felt so free.

Cathy woke up exhausted, starving and in great pain from her blistered hands and her twisted knee.

Moonlight had already woken, and was standing nearby, munching on some ferns.

"Moonlight?"

The unicorn turned towards her. *Cathy, you are hurt. I can sense great pain.*

"I landed badly getting over the gate last night."

Moonlight walked over to her, and bent down onto his knees. *Climb on my back, there is a pond nearby.*

"A pond? What good will that do?" Cathy asked as she pulled herself onto Moonlight's back.

After a few minutes, Cathy noticed a strong musty smell. She wrinkled her nose in distaste and grimaced when she realised that the smell was coming from the pond.

She climbed down, and stood at the edge of the water. The pond was thick with a fine green algae, and the small rainbow-coloured swirls on the surface told her that the water was far from unpolluted. Tired-looking weeds and ferns grew around the edge.

Watch closely, Moonlight said.

He bowed his head and dipped his horn into the water. As Cathy watched, the oily surface broke up and the algae disintegrated. Within a minute the water was pure and clear.

Cathy laughed. "That's fantastic! How did you do that?"

Moonlight winked at her. *Magic. Now, dip your hands in the water.*

She did so, placing them palm down. She felt a strange tingling sensation in her hands, and when she raised them again, the blisters and cuts had healed.

Cathy stepped tentatively into the pond, wading out until the water was up to her waist, and suddenly the pain in her knee was gone. Laughing, she scooped up some water in her hands and threw it into the air. The fine spray made tiny rainbows in the morning sunlight.

"Is it okay to drink?" Cathy asked.

Of course. The water can cure most illnesses. Some say that it can even bring back those who have just died.

She sipped at the water, and found it to be incredibly pure. It seemed to evaporate as she swallowed it, and then even her pangs of hunger began to fade. She felt refreshed and renewed, the exhaustion draining completely from her body.

Cathy bounded out of the water with energy she never knew she had, and hugged the unicorn. Then Moonlight dipped his head to drink.

ψ   ψ   ψ

Roger Brannigan had received a phone call from the police at one o'clock in the morning. They'd left about four, and he still hadn't slept.

How could this have happened? He asked himself for the hundredth time since discovering that Moonlight was missing. How is this possible?

When Emil Feyerman arrived back at Furlongs, Brannigan flew at him in a rage.

"He's gone! You bloody fool!"

Feyerman staggered back in shock. "What are you talking about?"

"The unicorn! Someone took him last night, while you were away! I thought you were supposed to be looking after him!"

Feyerman swallowed, shaking his head. "No. I don't believe it."

Brannigan grabbed the scientist by the arm and dragged him through the house out to the stable, where the bolt and padlock were lying on the ground.

"Who did this?" Feyerman asked.

"The girl. Cathy Donnelly. The police came here answering an alarm call, and they saw her on the unicorn's back, running over the fields."

"That's impossible. He could barely stand."

"He did more than stand. The police cornered them at the top of the field, and the unicorn leapt over the wall in one bound."

Feyerman bit his lip. "Did they see him? I mean, do they know he's not just a horse?"

Brannigan let out an angry breath. "Yes. They know. They were also very curious as to why you've got all that equipment in the stable. We are in a lot of trouble."

Feyerman smiled wickedly. "What do you mean *we*? This is your house, it's your unicorn. I've no idea what you're talking about."

Brannigan grabbed Feyerman by the lapels. "Listen very carefully, Feyerman. I've already told the police that you were staying here. They've seen your notes. All the equipment in there is yours. Now if you try to back out of this, I'll ruin you, is that clear?"

The scientist angrily pushed himself away. "Crystal."

Brannigan raked his hands though his hair. "They don't know who the girl is, and I've said I have no idea, but the description matches the Donnelly girl."

"So what now?"

"Find her, and the unicorn. I want the unicorn back here. As for the girl, I don't care."

The scientist looked around the stable. "Damn. I suppose the gardai searched this place? Did they take anything as evidence?"

"I don't know."

"I had a case with blood and tissue samples, it's not here." He searched the stable, then noticed a case under the desk. "No, here it is."

He reached down and grabbed it, and saw to his horror a deep horseshoe print in the case. It was completely crushed.

"That blasted unicorn! He knew what was in this!"

"What was it?" Brannigan asked.

"The only blood and tissue samples I'd taken from him. They're useless." He let the case drop to the floor. "Without live tissue samples we'll never be able to create another unicorn."

"Then find him. I don't care what it takes."

"Even if I have to kill him to get the samples?"

Brannigan turned away. "Whatever you have to do."

CHAPTER XI

"They'll come looking for us," Cathy said.

I know. Do you know of anywhere we might hide?

She shrugged. "There could be lots of places where they'll never find us, but I wouldn't have a clue where to start looking."

We are safe for now. Tell me about the scientist.

"I don't like him," Cathy said. "He seems pretty ruthless. Brannigan is worse, though. They're both obsessed by money."

Money, Moonlight said. *Money is one of the modern magics, Cathy. A promise to pay the bearer the equivalent in gold. Do you have much money?*

"Not much. Enough to keep us going for a while."

But not enough to last forever. What will happen when the money runs out?

"I don't know, Moonlight. We can eat for free, I'm sure there are berries and nuts and things in the forest, but I'll still need clothes and things like that."

Why are you giving up your old life for me?

"I was never happy. At least, I haven't been since my

grandparents went to England. I was happy on the farm, with you."

I think you'll find that your happiness was within yourself. When you began to look after me, when you stopped thinking of yourself first, then you became happier with yourself. Self-awareness is the first step to happiness.

Cathy wasn't sure how to take this. It seemed very profound coming from what was basically a horse with a horn on its head. No, she reminded herself, Moonlight is much more than that.

"What will happen to you?" Cathy asked.

Some day I'll mate, and produce offspring. And some day I'll die. That happens to every living thing.

"If you mate, what will your children be?"

Unicorns – Dr Feyerman would call it a dominant strain.

"And you can mate with any ordinary horse?"

Not just any horse, Moonlight said. *It must be female.*

Cathy nodded reflectively, then paused. "Very funny, Moonlight. I never thought you were the joking kind."

You just don't know how to see my smiles.

"If there were wild horses in Ireland, you would be able to start a herd of unicorns."

Yes, I'd like that. It is lonely being the only magical creature in the world.

Cathy opened her bag and pulled out her remaining sandwiches. "Damian told me that Dr Feyerman cloned you from a cell of a frozen prehistoric horse. In a way, you're like me. My father died before I was born too. And my mother is dead too."

It is not good to grow up without your parents, but if that is the situation then it is possible to become a much stronger person.

Cathy stood up and handed Moonlight an apple. He nibbled at it as she held it. "Moonlight, how did all this happen? Did you choose me, or did I choose you?"

We both needed someone. That is the way all the best friendships start.

ψ   ψ   ψ

They left the pond a few hours later, and Cathy noticed that the ferns and reeds in the pond seemed somehow greener, more full of life.

They walked side by side through the forest. Moonlight told Cathy which berries and fungi were edible, and which were poisonous. He told her how to make an edible stew from nettles, and how to find nourishment from the buds of certain wild flowers.

Cathy was amazed at the unicorn's knowledge. There seemed to be no end to his wise advice and tales. His stories of the old world were perfectly suited to the modern world, though Cathy suspected that he was selecting the stories deliberately.

"Moonlight, you said before that you have a sort of race memory, but this goes beyond that, doesn't it? Can you remember your past life?"

I don't know how long ago it was. Tonight I will examine the stars, and see how much their positions have changed.

"You can do that?"

I have a good memory, Moonlight said. *Now, sit. Rest here and I'll tell you my story.*

ψ   ψ   ψ

You must remember that when I last lived the pyramids of Egypt had not been built, nor had Ireland's legendary New Grange. This was many thousands of years before the time of Christ.

It was a time of war. We unicorns rarely fought, but humans have always done so. There was a king called Hrolf who led his people on bloodthirsty excursions through what is now known as Europe. He was wise in the ways of magic, and had the ability to cause his enemies to feel great fear from a long way off.

Often, by the time Hrolf had marched to the land of his enemies, they would already have fled or killed themselves in terror.

Hrolf was a madman: He killed the weak and elderly, and put many new-born babies to the sword just for his own pleasure at watching them die. His warriors were terrified of him, afraid of what might happen if they were to disobey. The civilians of Hrolf's land were relieved when he marched on another people, for that meant that their own suffering would cease for a short time.

But Hrolf himself was not without fear. He sent his men to slay any herd of unicorns they saw, for he knew that we were much more powerful than he.

In a few short years, only a small band of unicorns survived. I was the youngest of them, and I was arrogant. I thought that I would be able to stop Hrolf by myself.

When Hrolf's men managed to find our herd, I fought

89

viciously, killing many of the men. We escaped, but the herd leaders, though grateful that my actions had spared their lives, said that fighting was not the unicorn way.

I was banished, but I was still young enough not to care. I thought that I could live without them, but as the years passed I began to remember the comfort of friends. I decided to return, and spent almost a year following the signs of the herd.

And when I found them, I grieved, for all that was left was rotting corpses. Their heads had been removed, for even after death the horn of a unicorn is still capable of great magic.

It had been Hrolf and his warriors who slaughtered them, and realising this I found myself angry once again. Hrolf had wiped out my species, and I wanted revenge.

I went to Hrolf's land, moving only at night when my powers were stronger, and hiding during the day.

Hrolf lived in the main province of his land, in the centre of a small citadel. There was no way for me to get to him, so I waited.

I watched the citadel for months before I saw a convoy of men leaving, preparing for another war. Hrolf, as was his style, was at the lead.

I kept on a parallel course during that first day, but when the cold winter night fell I approached the camp.

I killed two of Hrolf's guards before they could alert the others to my presence, then I left.

The next day, Hrolf was angry at the guards' deaths. He ordered a search, but I eluded them.

That night I did the same, and for many days after. The men

became scared, thinking that some demon had come among them, but Hrolf scoffed at their superstitions, and forbade them to return to the citadel.

Soon less than half their number remained. When the winter came, I was even better protected – they could not see the white of my coat against the snow. I began to attack the scout parties, sometimes five or six men at a time. None ever escaped to warn the others.

Then the time came when there were only six left, including Hrolf. Still he refused to return to the citadel, though his men argued with him and threatened him, then pleaded and begged, knowing that they were lost. Even if I had not attacked again, they could not have posed a threat to their enemies.

And I did attack again. It was a bright morning, early spring. I attacked as they slept. I left only Hrolf alive.

He was still not afraid, and tried to use his power on me. But I was raging at the destruction of my own people: his power was useless.

Then I approached him, and ended his reign of terror forever.

ψ   ψ   ψ

"You killed him," Cathy said. She was astonished that this gentle animal was capable of so much destruction.

No, I wounded him, but let him live. I forced him back to his citadel. It took months, and I had to be on my guard at all times, but eventually we reached his homeland.

And everything had been destroyed. While Hrolf and his warriors had been away, his enemies had stormed the city and razed it to the ground.

Then Hrolf realised that I had only done to him what he had done to me. We were both alone. We spent the rest of the year together, not as prisoner and jailer, but as two who are bound by their mutual loss.

I was foolish. I thought that Hrolf had learned humility. But he was merely biding his time. One night while I slept he attacked a traveller, and took his sword. He came back to me, and slashed me with the stolen weapon.

I fought, but the wounds were deep. He defeated me easily, though I suspect that he died shortly afterwards, for I had stabbed him in the chest with my horn.

The last thing I remember was Hrolf hacking at my neck. I was the last of the unicorns, and he wanted my head as a symbol of his triumph.

Cathy shivered. She had been engrossed in Moonlight's story, and had not noticed that it was growing dark.

"I thought that you were going to give me a moral at the end of the story," she said.

There is no moral, except that which you take for yourself. What does the story mean to you?

She thought silently for a few minutes before answering. "I could say that it means that revenge is not the best motive, or that people should resist oppression, but all I can really think of is that your story shows that even a unicorn can be evil."

And is that what you think? That I was evil?

"You killed Hrolf's men, even though they were only acting out of fear. That was wrong."

But was it evil?

"I want to say that no, it wasn't evil, but I can't. You had plenty of time to think about what had happened. You could have had revenge on Hrolf without killing his men. It was evil, and I'm sorry if you hate me for thinking that, but that's the way it is."

Moonlight walked over to Cathy and lay down. He put his head in her lap and closed his eyes.

Cathy, to answer your earlier question ... You asked me if I chose you or if you chose me. The answer is simple. I chose you. You are the purest of the pure: selfless, noble, virtuous, innocent. Legend tells us that only the good can speak with the unicorns, and in a way that is true. Only the good are chosen by the unicorns to speak with them. Unicorns are said to be pure, but that is merely the reflection of their companions. We can be good or evil, just like humans.

Cathy stroked Moonlight's mane. "Moonlight, why are you telling me all this?"

Because before all this is over, you will need every ounce of goodness to save me and yourself. There are dark times ahead, I can feel them coming. There will be a war, Cathy. And you and I must be together to lead the good to victory.

CHAPTER XII

" I want a helicopter and weighted nets," Feyerman
said. "I want men with rifles and tranquilliser guns."

Brannigan nodded. "Anything you want. You'll get it."

"Infra-red binoculars and recent satellite photos of the
Wicklow mountains."

"The photos will be tough, but I'll do what I can. The
binoculars are no problem."

The men were in Brannigan's study, looking at a de-
tailed Ordnance Survey map of Wicklow, trying to guess
where the unicorn could have gone.

"I want him brought back at whatever cost. It's only a
matter of time before someone else spots the unicorn. I've
managed to convince the police that it was an ordinary
horse. I suggested that the girl must have fixed the horn
to his head as part of some deranged fantasy."

Feyerman nodded. "Good. That'll have them wasting
their time checking the hospitals too. What about the
girl's aunt?"

"I had the secretary phone her, asking for Cathy. The
aunt thinks that Cathy is spending the weekend with a
friend. She's expecting her back tomorrow after school.

Once she doesn't turn up, all hell is going to break loose. When she's reported missing, the aunt will give her photo to the gardai. They will circulate it to all the local branches, and the boys in blue in Dunlavin will recognise her."

"They'll find out that she was working with you in Lowlands."

"That can't be helped. We'll say that she must have known that we took Moonlight here, and she'd grown very attached to him since his birth."

Feyerman rubbed his tired eyes with his knuckles, and stifled a yawn. "Anything else that might help?"

"Just that Cathy never got on with her aunt. Running away from home is par for the course with such a relationship."

"All right. How soon can you get me the equipment?"

"By noon tomorrow. I don't know about the satellite pictures. I have a friend in the MET office who could get them for me, but it'll take time to process the images."

"The helicopter will do for a start. I'll make a few passes over the mountains at first. It'll either scare them enough to make them move, in which case we'll have them, or they'll stay put, in which case we'll be able to track them with dogs."

Brannigan checked his watch. "All right. Get some sleep, you start first thing in the morning."

ψ   ψ   ψ

Even before she was fully awake, Cathy instinctively knew that it was a Monday. She yawned and stretched, then pushed herself up from her bed of soft grass. She ran her fingers through her hair, dislodging a small beetle that had tried to make a nest for itself.

Moonlight was nowhere to be seen, but Cathy wasn't worried. She knew that he was safe. She opened her bag and emptied its contents onto the ground. There were still a few sandwiches remaining, though they were a bit stale. She wondered whether or not to throw them away, but decided not to waste them.

The peanut butter and banana sandwiches had somehow ended up in the bottom of her bag, and had been squashed into an unappealing paste, but she ate them anyway.

Having checked that there was no-one around, she quickly removed her jeans and sweatshirt, and replaced them with the cleaner, but badly wrinkled clothes from her bag. She washed her hands and face using water from the bottle they'd filled at the pond, and suddenly felt much better. There's nothing like a change of clothes and a wash to freshen you up, she said to herself.

So, it was Monday. By tonight her Aunt Margaret would be going mad with worry.

She thought about home, where there was a soft warm bed and plenty to eat, and she began to miss it. Maybe I should go home, she said to herself. Moonlight can look after himself, I should just get a bus –

All thoughts of going home disappeared as Moonlight

came dashing through the trees. His hooves threw up great clouds of dust, which were lit up by the shafts of sunlight that filtered through the branches.

Cathy smiled. Moonlight looked so powerful, so noble. But then she sensed his urgency, and knew that something was wrong.

Cathy! We must go, they're coming!

She gathered up her things and stuffed them into her bag. She ran to Moonlight and climbed quickly onto his back. As soon as she was settled, the unicorn galloped away.

"What's wrong, Moonlight?" She asked, ducking her head to avoid a low branch.

I can sense them coming, Cathy. They're flying! Dr Feyerman is with them, and he is very desperate.

"Flying ... Brannigan has a helicopter. It has a set of rotating blades on top."

It's coming from the west.

"But they'll never find us here," Cathy said. "The trees provide good cover."

They have a machine that senses heat patterns – I can read it in Feyerman's mind.

Then Cathy heard the helicopter itself. The sound was faint, but getting louder.

Hold on, Cathy. We're coming to the edge of the forest.

They broke out of the darkness and into a green field. Far above them, the helicopter turned in their direction.

Moonlight thundered across the field, Cathy hanging onto his mane and trying to grip with her legs.

The helicopter swooped down, and came alongside them. Moonlight suddenly turned, dashing away from it. Cathy almost fell off, but fear gave her the strength to hold on.

The helicopter matched their pace, following ten metres behind them. Through the roar of the blades they heard someone call out through a loudhailer.

"Stop! Cathy, this is Dr Feyerman! If you don't stop willingly we will be forced to stop you!"

"Keep going, Moonlight!"

Of course. They won't catch us, that machine can't keep going forever.

"Can you?"

If I need to.

Ψ   Ψ   Ψ

In the helicopter, Feyerman turned to two men who were holding a lead-weighted steel net. "Get ready. Once we're over them, drop it."

He tapped the pilot on the shoulder. "Get over them and drop to four metres."

The pilot nodded, and pushed forward on the control stick.

Ψ   Ψ   Ψ

The shadow of the helicopter passed over Cathy, and she ducked instinctively.

Then she felt something heavy drop onto them, and they were falling.

It was only luck that prevented Cathy from breaking her neck as she tumbled to the ground. She was thrown from Moonlight's back, but the heavy net prevented her from flying too far forward. She landed heavily on her back, winded.

ψ   ψ   ψ

Feyerman ordered the pilot to land the helicopter beside the unicorn. He was amazed at Moonlight's speed. He guessed that the unicorn had been travelling at over a hundred kilometres an hour.

As soon as the small helicopter's blades had slowed, Feyerman climbed out and walked over to Moonlight and Cathy.

He sighed heavily. "You were very foolish, young lady. You could have been killed."

Cathy was still too badly winded to talk, but she managed a scowl.

Feyerman examined Moonlight closely. "We meet again, my friend. Nothing broken, I hope. We'll soon have you back in the stable, where you belong."

He prodded the unicorn with his foot. "You didn't really think you could outrun the helicopter, did you?"

Cathy realised that Feyerman was talking to her, not to Moonlight. Of course, she said to herself, Moonlight's never communicated with him. He doesn't think that Moonlight has any more intelligence than an average horse.

"What are you going to do about me?" she asked.

"We're going to send you home, Cathy."

"I'll tell everyone that Moonlight's a unicorn. You wouldn't like that, would you?"

He smiled wickedly. "Don't threaten me, you're not in any position to do so. What you *are* in, however, is a lot of trouble. Running away from home, breaking and entering, theft of a valuable experimental animal. I, on the other hand, have done nothing illegal."

Cathy tried to get to her feet, but she found that she was entangled in the net and could barely move. "A valuable experimental animal! Is that all Moonlight is to you?"

He looked shocked. "Of course not! He's much, much more than that!" His shocked expression faded to be replaced by an evil grin. "Moonlight is worth a lot of money, Cathy. More money than you could possibly imagine."

Ψ   Ψ   Ψ

The scientist returned to the helicopter, and instructed the pilot to radio for a truck with a horsebox and return home.

The pilot strained to see past Feyerman. "That ... thing. Is it what I think it is?"

"That depends. What do you think it is?"

"A unicorn. Is it real?"

Feyerman laughed. It was the sort of laugh that suggested that such questions were best left unasked. "Oh, it's real, all right. But it's only a horse. That girl is a bit, well, unbalanced, shall we say? She had this fantasy that Moonlight was really a unicorn. The horn is made of papier-mâché, and she painted the tail and mane gold with a spray can." He sighed. "It's very sad, really. This isn't the first time she's done something like this."

The pilot nodded, believing the scientist's story. "It seems a bit drastic, though. I mean, using a helicopter and weighted nets to catch a runaway girl."

Feyerman glared at him. "It seems drastic, does it? Tell me, how much is Roger Brannigan paying you?"

The pilot brightened, suddenly aware that, if he played his cards right and kept his mouth shut, the scientist might offer to increase his wages. "Four hundred a week, Doctor," he lied. It was really only three hundred pounds a week, but you never knew what sort of an increase you might get.

"Four hundred a week, eh?" Feyerman said, smiling kindly. "Well, how about I get Mr Brannigan to halve your wages? Or would you prefer to forget everything you've seen here today?"

The pilot swallowed. "Forget what?"

"Good man. You catch on quick. Now do as I told you." He turned to the two other men in the helicopter. "You heard that. It applies to all of you."

The men looked at one another and grumbled, but they had families to provide for, and wisely decided to forget about the unicorn.

ψ   ψ   ψ

With difficulty, Cathy turned on her side and looked at the unicorn. "Moonlight? Are you all right?"

I have some minor bruising, but otherwise I'm fine. And you?

"I'm okay. I thought you said they wouldn't catch us?"

I was wrong. I didn't know about the net.

"What will they do to us?"

Nothing. We will escape.

"Let's hope you're not wrong about *that*. Can you move?"

No. My legs are tangled in the net.

"Well, how about if I –"

Moonlight interrupted her. *Quiet! The doctor is approaching. He must not discover that you can communicate with me.*

Cathy turned, and saw Feyerman walking towards them. She gasped. The scientist was carrying a rifle.

CHAPTER XIII

"This," said the scientist patting the rifle, "is to make sure that Moonlight doesn't try to run away again."

"What will happen to him?" Cathy asked.

"I'll take him back to the lab, and continue my studies."

"I don't understand," Cathy said. "Why are you studying him? Moonlight's just a horse with a golden horn. That's all unicorns are."

Feyerman raised an eyebrow in disbelief. "Is that so? Then why did you go to so much trouble to free him?"

Cathy said nothing.

"In fact, what I really want to know is how you discovered his whereabouts. No-one at Lowlands knew that we had taken him to Furlongs, not even that insufferable Damian Corscadden."

"I guessed," Cathy said. "It seemed the most obvious place."

"Really? Somehow I don't believe you, Miss Donnelly." He patted the rifle again. "Now, tell me the truth. I suspect that there's more to this beast than you're letting on."

"Go ahead, shoot me. Then you'll never find out."

She heard Moonlight's voice in her head. *Cathy, we need*

to gain some time. Ask him again about his plans.

"What sort of studies were you doing on him? I saw all the tubes and things in the stable, but I couldn't work out what they were for."

Feyerman sat down on the grass beside Cathy. If it hadn't been for the steel net, she would have lashed out at him.

Behind them the helicopter's engines began to whine, the blades whirling faster.

"They're going to get a truck and horsebox, Cathy. We're going home. But in answer to your question, I was monitoring Moonlight's amazing growth rate. Do you realise that he has reached maturity in less than five months? Every day I took a photo of him, always from the same angle and with Moonlight in the same position. Put together they make a fascinating display. You can actually see him growing."

"I have another question: Why did you only make one unicorn? You could have made hundreds."

"Who says I *didn't* make hundreds? Don't worry, there are a lot more unicorns where Moonlight came from."

He's lying, Cathy. If there were any others I would be able to sense them.

Cathy smiled wickedly. "Well, if you did make more unicorns, then where are they? Why would you go to so much trouble getting Moonlight back?"

"You have called my bluff. Moonlight is – so far – the only one."

"But why are you doing all this?" Cathy asked.

Feyerman shrugged. "Partly from curiosity, partly from the fame it will undoubtedly bring me, but mostly I'm doing it for the money."

Cathy scowled. "Money, money, money. That's all you and Brannigan ever think about. You must have enough money to keep you going for the rest of your life. Why do you want more?"

"One can never have enough money, Cathy. When you're older you'll understand that too."

"Never. I'll never think like that."

Behind them, the helicopter rose into the air and disappeared over the hills.

Feyerman watched it go, then turned back to Cathy. "My family were moderately wealthy, I'm not going to pretend they weren't. It would be easy to lie and say that I had nothing as a child, and as such I want as much as I can get now, but that wouldn't be true. I went to college, studied medicine for a couple of years, but what I was really interested in was genetics. Did you know that the presence of DNA was only discovered in 1952?"

Cathy shook her head, wondering where all this was leading.

"Imagine, 1952! And for thousands of years scientists tried to understand the way people are. DNA is ... You do know what DNA is, don't you?"

"Sort of. It's like a pattern that can duplicate itself. It defines the way we grow."

Feyerman nodded. "Very good. Every cell in your body contains a copy of your DNA – deoxyribonucleic acid –

and everyone's DNA is completely unique. Back about ten years ago, people thought that if they could fully analyse and decode DNA then it would be a better method of identification than fingerprinting. It can be done now, of course. If, for example, the police wanted to ascertain that you were the one who broke into Brannigan's stable, they'd search the stable until they found some skin or hair samples, and match them with yours."

Cathy nodded. "I suppose that one day they'll have everyone's DNA on computer, so they can find out who committed any crime, just by matching the DNA."

"Very good again. You're no fool, Miss Donnelly. Upon someone's birth a sample of their blood could be taken, and the DNA structure logged with the rest of their details."

Keep him talking, Cathy. The longer he talks, the more time we'll have to think of something.

"What if ... " Cathy paused, and tried to look as though she was coming up with the right words, while she was really trying to think of something clever to ask. "What if you had all that, and compared the DNA of everyone in the world with everyone else? If the DNA matched would that mean that the people were identical?"

"Hmm ... Good question. Not necessarily. You see, DNA instructs our bodies on the way to grow, but that doesn't mean that our bodies *will* grow what way. Something else might affect that."

"Like what?" Cathy asked.

"A disease or an accident."

"But if you examine a baby's DNA you can tell how tall it will be, whether it will be fat or thin, blond or dark, that sort of thing?"

"Within a very high percentage, yes."

"But can you change someone's DNA then, the way you did with Moonlight before he was born?"

The scientist nodded. "Yes. Once something like that is fully understood, all you need to do is re-program the DNA."

"That way you could make people be anything you wanted. You could build athletes who could run faster than anyone else, or make a whole bunch of very strong people."

"Exactly. The possibilities are limitless. One real application would be, in the far future of course, to build people with extremely high intelligence and powerful bodies who would be able to adapt to the dangerous conditions of another planet."

"So science has an answer for everything, doesn't it?"

Feyerman looked at Moonlight, and shook his head. "No, not everything."

Ψ   Ψ   Ψ

Less than an hour later, they saw a Land Rover coming across the field. It was towing a horsebox. Feyerman stood up and stretched.

"Well, Cathy, that was quite a conversation. Perhaps genetics is something you should think about for a career for yourself. You certainly have the grasp of the concepts."

"Please don't hurt Moonlight," Cathy said.

He smiled. "Sometimes, in the name of science, the innocent must suffer."

"But that's not fair!"

"No, it's not fair. But that's life."

CHAPTER XIV

Halfway across the field, the Land Rover stopped, its wheels still turning, throwing up great clumps of mud.

Muttering to himself in disgust, Feyerman walked over. "What's the trouble, Mr Corscadden?"

Damian rolled down the window and leaned out. "I'm stuck. Sorry, the field didn't *look* this muddy."

"Put it into four-wheel drive," Feyerman suggested. "That should give you enough power."

Damian did so, and pressed down hard on the accelerator. This had the effect of digging the Land Rover deeper into the mud.

"Get out," Feyerman said. "I'll do it."

Damian climbed out and held the door open for Dr Feyerman. He looked over to where Cathy and Moonlight were still entangled in the net.

Feyerman had no more luck with the Land Rover than Damian.

"What about the horse?" Damian asked. "He should be able to get enough traction to get us out. And I'll unhitch the horsebox, its weight is keeping us back."

"All right," the scientist said, climbing down from the driver's seat. "Come with me. I've a few things to explain about Moonlight."

ψ ψ ψ

Damian couldn't believe what he was looking at. "The last time I saw Moonlight he was tiny! And this ... The horn, the golden mane! It's incredible!"

"Not incredible, Mr Corscadden. Merely science."

"Cathy, it's good to see you again, though I never thought we'd meet like this. Are you all right?"

Cathy nodded. "I'm okay, no thanks to –"

Feyerman interrupted her. "Enough! Corscadden, get the harness from the Land Rover. We'll need to make sure that Moonlight doesn't try to escape."

As Damian walked away, the scientist fumbled with the net, and managed to free Cathy. "I would advise you to stay where you are, Cathy. You can't outrun the Land Rover."

Cathy said nothing. In fact, she didn't even hear him. She was communicating with Moonlight. You did that, didn't you? she thought. You made the Land Rover get stuck. We rode over that part of the field, and there was no mud.

You are right, it was my doing. But it will be their undoing.

Damian arrived back, and handed the harness to Dr Feyerman. "Don't give it to me, you fool! Here, I'll release the unicorn's head, you put the harness on him."

"Why me?"

"Because he might be vicious enough to bite, and that horn looks sharp."

"Thanks a lot," Damian muttered.

Moonlight offered no resistance when they put the harness on him. Damian held onto the unicorn while the scientist freed him from the net.

When Moonlight got to his feet, Damian led him back to the Land Rover, while the scientist kept a hold on Cathy.

Damian tied a heavy blue nylon rope around Moonlight, tied the other end to the front of the Land Rover's chassis, and unhitched the horsebox.

He climbed into the driver's seat and revved up the engine.

Moonlight knew what was expected of him. He walked forward, slowly at first, taking up the slack in the rope. Then he began to strain, the muscles on his back and legs standing out sharply against his normally smooth coat.

The Land Rover began to inch forward.

Moonlight, Cathy thought, make it easy on yourself. Just make the ground hard again.

I can't. If I do that they'll notice.

Soon the Land Rover was clear of the muddy patch. Damian untied Moonlight and led him to the horsebox. It was a lot lighter than the Land Rover, but as it lacked an engine Moonlight had to do all the work for himself.

Damian hitched the horsebox back to the Land Rover, and tried to lead Moonlight inside, but the unicorn resisted. He wasn't violent, he just refused to go in.

"For God's sake!" Feyerman shouted. He let go of Cathy to help Damian.

Now, run Cathy! But let them catch you!

Cathy paused for a second, then turned and fled. Feyerman saw her, and ordered Damian to give chase.

She didn't have to let Damian catch her – she was still weak from the fall, and couldn't run too fast anyway. Damian grabbed Cathy by the arm, and brought her back to the Land Rover. "I'm sorry about this, Cathy," he said quietly. "I have to do what he says."

He opened the door and pushed her inside. "Now stay there!" he growled, but he winked at the same time and pointed to the keys that were still dangling in the ignition. "Good luck," he whispered.

Damian walked back to the scientist, and this time Moonlight offered only token resistance. Damian and Feyerman pushed up the ramp and slid the bolts shut.

"Right," Feyerman said. "Let's get back –"

Suddenly the Land Rover's engine roared into life. With a jerk, the vehicle began to move, slowly at first, but with increasing speed.

Raging, Feyerman ran after it as best as he could. Damian followed, smiling to himself. "Remember, Cathy, ease off the clutch *gently*," he said quietly.

Ψ   Ψ   Ψ

Cathy bumped about in the driver's seat, desperately trying to remember what Damian had taught her about driving. She was travelling at over thirty kilometres an hour, puzzled by the deafening whine from the engine, before she remembered to move into second gear.

"Moonlight? Are you all right back there?"

Don't worry about me. Just concentrate on not hitting anything.

She grinned. "Hey, I trusted you when we were dashing through the forest, didn't I?"

Yes, but I'm qualified to dash through the forest.

"Where will we go?" Cathy asked.

We can't go too far. I'm sure they'll be looking out for the vehicle.

"I know, I'll leave it somewhere it could be stolen."

First, let's get onto the road, Moonlight said.

"We *are* on the road! We've been on the road for the last five minutes!"

Sorry, it's just the way the vehicle keeps jerking. I thought we were crossing an endless series of ditches.

ψ　　ψ　　ψ

The Land Rover sped along the dual carriageway. "The other drivers keep looking at me," Cathy said.

Are you sure you're driving on the right side of the road?

"I'm not."

You're not?

"No, I'm driving on the left."

Don't do that. It's unnerving back here. I can't see what you're doing.

"Believe me, you don't want to see." She paused.

"There's a signpost. It looks like we're going towards Carlow."

Who?

"Carlow, it's a place. I think we should head for the west, though. I wonder how we get there?"

Stop when you find somewhere sheltered, Cathy. We can ride the rest of the way.

They stopped after about five minutes, in a narrow side-road. Cathy struggled with the bolts on the ramp, but finally managed to get them open. Moonlight staggered out, weaving from side to side a little.

I don't want to criticise your driving, Cathy, but I think it might have been better if you had been in the horsebox and I had been driving the vehicle.

She scowled at him. "Very funny, Moonlight. What should we do now?"

We should get away from here as fast as possible. Is there anything in the vehicle that we could use?

"The only useful thing is a map of the country."

Good. There's a saddle in the horsebox. That should make things a bit more comfortable for you.

"I'll put the hazard lights on," Cathy said. "Drivers always do that when a car's broken down, or when they want to park illegally."

Cathy did so, noticing the way Moonlight kept well back from the Land Rover while she fiddled with the various switches. After switching on the radio and washing the windows, she found the hazard lights.

Then, not without some difficulty, she lifted the saddle

onto Moonlight's back. Moonlight complained that it didn't feel right, so Cathy took it off and turned it around. *That's better*, Moonlight said.

Cathy fastened the buckles as well as she could, and climbed into the saddle. She had to admit, it was a lot more comfortable than riding bareback.

Moonlight broke into an easy trot. The wind in her hair and face felt so good to Cathy.

They were free again.

CHAPTER XV

It was a cold night in the woods, but that wasn't what bothered Cathy. She was starving. She'd finished the last of her sandwiches and apples that morning, hoping that they'd find something on the way, but her conscious decision to avoid any major towns kept them well away from anywhere that sold food.

We can go for food now, Cathy, Moonlight said.

"No, it's too late. Most shops close at six. It's only in the larger towns that they stay open. Can't you use your magic to make some food?"

It doesn't work like that, Cathy. Sorry.

She sighed. "It's okay. I can wait till morning."

No, you must have food. Come with me. Moonlight walked off into the woods.

"Where are we going?" Cathy asked.

Quiet. We don't want to frighten them.

"Frighten who?" she whispered.

The rabbits. There are some in a field nearby, I can sense them.

"Rabbits! Moonlight, I couldn't kill and eat a harmless little bunny! Besides, I'd need to make a fire to cook it."

Moonlight turned back to Cathy and gave her a look of disbelief. *I wasn't suggesting that, Cathy. Think about it.*

Cathy frowned in puzzlement, then shook her head. "People can't think on an empty stomach, Moonlight. Well known fact. It's all right for *you*, you can eat grass."

Rabbits are nocturnal. Therefore they eat at night. We will follow them and find where they eat. There is a farm nearby, there could be carrots and lettuce.

"No hope of a pizza, then?"

What's a pizza?

Cathy grinned. "Aha! At last I've found something you don't know about! A pizza is a sort of large, round, flat, bready thing, with a cheese and tomato base and anything you like as a topping."

Well, think of this as a pizza without the bread, cheese or tomato, and with a carrot and lettuce topping.

"Now I really *am* starving."

It's a pity that humans never learned to eat grass, Moonlight said. *Imagine what that would do to society. Some animals eat only grass. They don't need coffee in the morning and sandwiches for lunch. They certainly don't need chocolate or ice cream.*

"Well, it sounds terribly dull to me, eating grass all the time."

It is, but they don't know that. Life would be a lot simpler without canned drinks and French fries and pizzas and Christmas cake and –

"Will you stop talking about food? You're torturing me!"

I'm sorry. Moonlight stopped, raised his head and sniffed. *They're nearby.*

Cathy took out her torch. "Will the light frighten them?"

Normally, yes, but I'll try to keep them calm.

She switched on the torch and pointed it at the field in front of her. The beam showed dozens of small brown rabbits, bounding and leaping. They took no notice of Cathy and Moonlight.

"They're gorgeous!" Cathy said.

I'm sure the local farmers don't think so.

"Aw, look! A baby bunny! He's so cute! Look at his little tail!"

Yes, marvellous. They're beginning to move, we'll follow them.

Ψ   Ψ   Ψ

They returned to the woods an hour later, laden with freshly pulled carrots and lettuce, leaving behind some very unusual rabbit tracks for the farmer to worry about.

Cathy checked the lettuce and carrots carefully for slugs and insects, and washed them in the last of the bottled water before eating them.

Moonlight lay down to sleep, and Cathy curled up beside him. During the night, some of the more curious rabbits wandered into the woods. They could tell that Moonlight was a powerful animal, and they felt safe in his company. They gathered around. One of them even snuggled up to Cathy.

ψ   ψ   ψ

Margaret was in a state of panic. When Cathy had failed to turn up after school, Margaret had assumed that she was just delayed. At eight o'clock she was worried enough to call the school principal at home.

"Mrs Spencer? This is Margaret O'Toole, Cathy Donnelly's aunt."

"Yes, Ms O'Toole, how is Cathy then? Feeling better?"

"What? What do you mean?"

"Cathy didn't turn up for school today. I assumed that she was ill, or something."

Margaret bit her lip. "Oh God, no. She didn't turn up at all?"

"No. Are you telling me she's gone missing?"

"It looks like it. She left on Friday evening. She was spending the weekend with Julie, and said that she'd probably just go straight in to school today."

"And have you tried to contact Julie?"

Margaret felt herself growing cold. "Well, I don't know where she lives. I don't even know her second name."

"I don't *believe* this. Did you *ask* Cathy who this Julie was?"

"Well, no. I got the impression that she was a girl in Cathy's class. That's why I phoned you. I thought you could give me her phone number."

"Ms O'Toole, there is no Julie in Cathy's class. Do you have any idea where she could have gone?"

Margaret swallowed, the full significance of this had

just hit her. "No. There's nowhere. She doesn't really have any friends in Dublin."

Mrs Spencer took a deep breath. "You knew that, yet you still believed her when she said she was going to stay with someone for the weekend? All right. Phone the police, tell them that Cathy's been missing since Friday night. Give them a description, they'll want to know what she's wearing, how much money she has, anything she might have brought with her, that sort of thing. Phone me back if there's any news."

Margaret thanked the principal and put down the phone.

She stared at the phone for a full five minutes. Maybe I should give her another half an hour. If she doesn't turn up, I'll phone the police then. Or Stephen, he'll be able to help.

But Margaret was slowly coming to realise something that most people discover much earlier in life. Problems like this don't just go away – sooner or later you have to deal with them. And preferably sooner, because problems like this have a tendency to grow.

Ψ   Ψ   Ψ

Roger Brannigan and Dr Emil Feyerman were coming to the same conclusion. Feyerman had tried to blame Damian Corscadden for letting Cathy and Moonlight escape, but Brannigan wasn't going to let the scientist away that easily.

"You were in charge of the operation!" Brannigan

roared. "Your incompetence allowed them to escape!"

"We'll find them. They can't have gone far."

"The Land Rover was found at two o'clock this afternoon. It's now midnight. We know that Moonlight can travel at a comfortable seventy kilometres an hour, we've done enough tests. And he doesn't tire! That means we have a search radius of seven hundred kilometres, which, in case it has escaped your feeble mind, covers this entire country!"

"Sooner or later someone will spot them. It's just a matter of time."

"Feyerman, Cathy's aunt will have phoned the police by now. By morning every police station in the country will have a photo of her. The police in Dunlavin will recognise her. What's more, they'll find out that she worked for us. It won't take them long to realise she's the one who stole Moonlight. Then there will be some very awkward questions."

The scientist tapped his fingers angrily on the desk. "Look, give it a rest, okay? I'm trying to work out a way to catch them myself. I don't need your amateur input. And speaking of amateurs, did the helicopter pilot or his men mention anything about the unicorn?"

"No, nothing. They looked pretty annoyed when they got back, though."

Feyerman nodded. "Good. They had a close enough look at Moonlight, but I threatened them with a salary cut if they mentioned it to anyone."

Brannigan closed his eyes and swore. "Wrong again.

You should have promised them a bonus if they kept quiet. Now I've got unhappy employees to deal with as well. All it takes is for one of them to sell the story to the press. I suppose you didn't get the blood and tissue samples?"

"No. I wanted to do that in the laboratory."

"You had the unicorn there for almost two hours, and you didn't get the samples. You realise that there's a strong possibility we'll never get another chance?"

"I know that."

Brannigan pointed to the door. "Get out, Feyerman. I want a completely foolproof method of capturing them by six tomorrow morning. Mess this up and you're history."

The scientist said nothing. He turned and left the room, slamming the door behind him. You're next, Brannigan, he said to himself. After I catch the unicorn, you're next.

Ψ   Ψ   Ψ

The dog handler resented being called out so early in the morning, but the money that Dr Feyerman had offered was enough to help him forget his lost sleep.

He was a tall, well-built man of fifty. His hands and forearms were covered in ugly scratches and scabs, which Feyerman attributed to the vicious dogs of which he was so proud.

"You realise, Mr Cullen, that this ... operation ... is strictly between us?"

The big man nodded. "Yeah, yeah. I do a lot of covert

operations." He grinned, showing several missing teeth.

Feyerman gazed at the dog handler's wide red face. "It goes without saying, of course, that if any of this gets out we'll deny all knowledge."

Cullen shrugged. "I'm used to that. Just tell me who you want caught."

"Not *who* – what. One of Mr Brannigan's prize racehorses has been stolen. Now, to be honest, we're not worried about the horse itself, it's getting on a bit and not really worth much, but it hasn't been gelded, and Mr Brannigan doesn't want any of his competitors to get access to his breeding stock."

The dog handler nodded. "A horse. Right. Never had much time for horses, myself. Too high and mighty, bloody smug animals. A dog is your best friend."

"So you think you can help us?"

"Yeah. I've got anything doggish you can think of. Bloodhounds that can track anything, greyhounds that could catch any horse. And – " he winked conspiratorially " – if you want someone seen to, there's nothing better than a good Rottweiler. If you catch my meaning."

Feyerman nodded. "I catch your meaning. What sort of money are we talking about?"

"Five grand per day, plus losses."

"Losses?"

"Anything happens to my dogs, they'll need to be replaced."

"Five thousand pounds a day, eh?" The scientist, who was used to dealing with services for money, shook his head. "Now, I don't think that's acceptable."

"Fair enough." Cullen turned and began to walk away.

Feyerman called him back. "Aren't you supposed to negotiate?"

"The way I see it, negotiation is over. I named a price, you refused. If you've got an offer, it'd better be pretty impressive to keep me here."

"If I were to pay you five thousand pounds a day, how do I know you'll bother to look at all? You could become rich just by sitting in the pub."

"So what do you say?"

"I'm offering you fifty thousand pounds to find that horse within the week. No expenses, no bonuses. Fail, however, and you get nothing. That's the way my employer does business. Take it or leave it."

"You want this horse just found, or brought back as well?"

"If you can't bring him back, just make sure that I can get to him."

"You want him alive or dead?"

Feyerman paused. There really was no need to keep Moonlight alive. As long as he had the blood samples, the scientist could easily create another unicorn. "It doesn't matter."

"I'll use the Rottweilers to bring him down," Cullen said. "They're about the most dangerous you can get. They could stop any horse. Be a pretty bloody sight, mind you."

Feyerman shrugged. "It's just a horse."

They closed the deal and shook hands. Cullen marched away, to prepare his dogs for the hunt. The scientist had given him Moonlight's old horse blanket from the stable at Furlongs, from which the bloodhounds could catch the scent.

Feyerman hadn't slept the night before. He'd sat up trying to work out a way to catch Moonlight, and if that failed a way to take as much as he could from Roger Brannigan before he left the country.

If he hadn't been so exhausted, Dr Feyerman might have remembered that Moonlight was accompanied by Cathy Donnelly. But it never occurred to him the damage a Rottweiler could do to a young girl.

CHAPTER XVI

Cathy and Moonlight strolled through the woods. Cathy was looking at the map they'd taken from the Land Rover, trying to figure out where they could hide.

Don't you miss your old life? Moonlight asked.

"Not really. Not yet, anyway. I can always go home once we find you somewhere safe."

I'm glad you think that way. It would be foolish to think that we could stay together forever. You are still very young, you have your whole life ahead of you.

"Do you think that there will ever be other unicorns?"

I hope so. This world of yours is in quite a mess. Without us the human race has become greedy, they think that this earth is theirs to do with as they will. Of course, there were wars and such before, but never of this scale.

"They say that there are enough nuclear weapons on earth to destroy the world hundreds of times over."

No single species should have that much power. Science should be used to help life, not to end it.

Ψ   Ψ   Ψ

At noon, they stopped to eat again.

"I'm getting pretty tired of carrots," Cathy said. "Maybe we should find a shop, or something."

Are there any towns nearby?

"There should be a small village about eleven kilometres north of here," Cathy said, peering at the map. "That's assuming that we're not totally useless at map reading."

Climb on, Cathy. We'll go look for the village.

"Wait a minute, we don't know which way is north."

It is noon, so the sun is at its peak. Since it rises in the east, and sinks in the west, then at its peak the sun is to the south.

Cathy smiled. "I should have thought of that."

Moonlight covered the eleven kilometres with ease. Cathy left him hidden in a clump of trees off the road, and walked into the village.

She found a small shop on the side of the road. In the window were faded cereal packets and plastic fruit. There was a newspaper rack hanging outside the door with yellowed, rain-soaked newspapers that were more than a year old.

Despite the neglected appearance of the shop, it was fairly well stocked. Cathy bought a bag of apples, a French loaf, half a pound of tomatoes, a carton of milk and a wedge of cheese. "We left the picnic stuff at home," she said to the aged man behind the counter.

The shopkeeper just nodded and said nothing. He took out his biro and added up the cost of the food on the back of a brown paper bag, then rang up "no sale" on the till.

As an afterthought, Cathy bought herself a Mars bar. She decided that she deserved a treat.

When she got back to the clump of trees, Moonlight was missing. Cathy stood still for a few minutes, looking around stupidly.

Then Moonlight walked casually back through the trees.

"Where were you? I thought something had happened! I said to wait here!"

I had to take care of business. Sorry.

"Business? What are you talking about?"

Cathy would never have imagined that a unicorn could look embarrassed, but Moonlight did a very good impression of it.

You know, business. A bowel movement.

She stared blankly at him.

I had to go to the toilet.

It was Cathy's turn to be embarrassed. "Well! You needn't be so forward about it!"

You did ask me. I see you got some food.

Cathy sat down and opened the plastic bag. "You want an apple?"

Moonlight nodded. Cathy tossed an apple towards the unicorn, but instead of catching it in his mouth, Moonlight speared it with his horn.

Cathy laughed. "That's brilliant! But now how are you going to eat it?"

Moonlight tossed his head up, dislodging the apple, and caught it in his mouth as it fell.

"You're pretty handy with that horn. Did unicorns always use them for fighting?"

No, mostly for defence. Some people – and some unicorns – think that the horn is just a symbol, but nature always has a reason for everything.

"Oh yeah? What about eyebrows? I've never been able to figure out what they're for."

They keep the sweat out of your eyes. It's conceivable that, in the far future when every environment is controlled, humans will lose their eyebrows.

"All right, then. Why do men have nipples?"

Moonlight stared blankly at her. *Such questions have troubled the most intelligent humans for a long time. No human knows the true answer to that.*

"Do you know?"

Of course. Unicorns know everything.

"Tell me, then. Why do men have nipples?"

He paused. *It's a secret.*

Cathy laughed. "You're a liar, Moonlight! Unicorns don't know everything."

No, but we do have a sense of humour.

This time, Cathy thought she could see the unicorn smile.

ψ   ψ   ψ

In the small side road where Cathy and Moonlight had abandoned the Land Rover, the dog handler patted his favourite bloodhound on the back. "All right, Oscar. See what you can get." He held the blanket to the dog's nose, then unclipped the leash.

Oscar immediately lowered his nose to the ground and began sniffing. It took him a couple of minutes to find the scent, but when he did he began speeding across the field like a four-legged vacuum cleaner.

Cullen climbed onto his motorbike and followed the bloodhound. Occasionally he had to call to the dog to wait while he went around a ditch, but otherwise they made good time.

He had been involved in searches similar to this before, and he knew that for every kilometre the bloodhound covered, it narrowed the chances of his quarry escaping.

It was late afternoon before they found where Moonlight and Cathy had slept the previous night. Oscar was getting tired, so Cullen took out his mobile phone and called his employees.

The men who worked for Cullen were driving along the country roads in a large van, doing their best to keep up with Cullen and Oscar. In the back of the van were two other bloodhounds and three Rottweilers. The dogs had not been fed since the previous day, and were becoming increasingly restless.

"Oscar's getting tired, lads. Get one of the others ready. We'll be waiting for you on the road."

"Any progress?" The driver asked.

"Yeah. We've found where the horse slept last night. There are footprints here. Whoever took the horse is running with him."

"So we can't use the Rottweilers to stop the horse, then."

"I don't see why not," Cullen said. "Feyerman sort of hinted that he wouldn't mind too much if the thieves were, em, punished, if you get my meaning."

"How much are we getting for all this? I want to be sure it's worth it. Remember that guy last year? Bruno almost killed him."

"If we find the horse within the week we're getting thirty thousand," Cullen lied. "And that's good money, from a legitimate businessman."

"All right, that's cool." The driver put down the phone and turned to look at the dogs. "Hungry, boys?"

The Rottweilers began to growl.

Ψ　　Ψ　　Ψ

When it started to rain, Cathy and Moonlight took shelter in the local public park. "I don't like all this waiting around," Cathy said. "Anybody could be following us."

Would you rather get wet?

"I'd rather that unicorns came with a built-in roof."

The rain will stop in a few minutes, we can move on then.

As Moonlight had predicted, the rain stopped in less than five minutes. The unicorn led Cathy over to the park's pond, dipped his horn in to purify the water, and suggested to Cathy that she refill the water bottle.

"Now what?" Cathy asked.

Before anyone else decides to go for an evening stroll in the park, I suggest that we find somewhere else to hide.

ψ   ψ   ψ

Oscar's replacement was almost exhausted by the time they found the place where Moonlight and Cathy had their picnic. There had been a heavy shower of rain, and the scent of the horse was almost gone, but the dog's keen sense of smell soon located the unicorn's droppings.

"Still fresh," Cullen muttered, nudging the pile of dung with his foot. "Can't be gone too far."

The van was waiting on the road. "Right, lads. They're somewhere around here. It's time to let Bruno and his mates out to play." He took out his phone and called Dr Feyerman.

ψ   ψ   ψ

Moonlight woke first. He could hear the dogs a long way off, but they were getting closer by the second. He backed nervously away from the sound.

They had tried to find a cave in the mountains, but had been forced to settle for shelter under a small rocky outcrop.

Wake up, Cathy, we're in trouble.

"Hmmm? What?" Cathy turned over onto her back, rubbing her eyes. "Moonlight, what's wrong?"

Dogs. There is a pack of dogs coming. They're looking for us.

She sat up. "Dogs? Well, we can outrun them, can't we?"

There is no time. We'll have to fight them. Get back against the rocks, don't let them get behind you.

Cathy swallowed. "How many minutes before they get here?"

None.

A large black Rottweiler crashed through the undergrowth. It stopped when it saw Moonlight, then began to advance slowly, snarling as it moved.

Two more appeared behind the first. They spread out, coming towards Moonlight from different angles.

The unicorn made a move to attack one of them, but as it backed away, the others came closer. Gradually, Moonlight found himself pinned against the rocks.

Cathy stood beside him, trembling. "Moonlight, stop them!"

The dog on the left leaped, his huge strong teeth aimed at Moonlight's throat. The unicorn turned and lashed out with his leg, knocking the dog backwards. At the same time, the dog on the right attacked, coming at Moonlight from behind.

Moonlight kicked out with both of his hind legs, smashing the Rottweiler into a tree.

The third dog attacked, landing heavily on Moonlight's back. Cathy screamed.

The unicorn turned, and tried to crush the dog against the rocky outcrop, but the first dog attacked again. It went for Moonlight's throat again, gripping with his powerful teeth.

Moonlight roared. Thrashing madly, he managed to dislodge the dog on his back. It circled around, and leaped again.

The unicorn turned, and impaled the dog on his horn. The dead Rottweiler slumped to the ground.

The dog at Moonlight's throat held its grip, and began slashing at the unicorn with its claws.

Without thinking, Cathy reached forward and grabbed the Rottweiler by the neck. The dog instantly let go of the unicorn and turned on her.

But before it could attack, Moonlight leaped forward, landing on the dog's back, killing it instantly.

Cathy stood shaking and crying. Moonlight was bleeding profusely from his wounds. He collapsed slowly to the ground.

People ... coming, Cathy ... Run. Save yourself.

"No, Moonlight! I won't leave you!"

But the unicorn lay still, his great chest rising and falling irregularly.

"Moonlight, wake up! Please! We've got to get away from here!"

"I'm afraid it's too late for that, Cathy."

Cathy turned. Standing behind her was Dr Emil Feyerman.

CHAPTER XVII

Three men appeared behind Feyerman. They went immediately to the dogs, but found that only one was still alive.

Cullen stood up. "This one'll have to be put down, Doc. This is going to cost you."

"Don't you remember our agreement, Mr Cullen? Fifty thousand, no expenses."

Cullen's men looked at each other. "Fifty thousand?" One said to Cullen. "You told us thirty."

Cullen glared at him. "Shut up." He walked towards the scientist, stopping only inches away. "You never told me that the thief was a girl. You led me to believe that there was some gang of international horse thieves. And this thing," he waved his arm to indicate Moonlight, "this is no horse."

Feyerman knew that he was seriously outclassed, and had no choice but to come up with a compromise. "All right. You've got a point. You say nothing about this, ever, and I'll raise the price to seventy-five thousand."

Cullen crossed his arms and shook his head slowly. "I don't know, Doc. Seems to me that I'd get a lot more than that from one of the papers for a story like this."

"You'd need to have proof."

"Sure we have proof. We could just take that thing with us."

"Over my dead body."

Cullen's hand flashed, and suddenly he was holding a large fishing knife. "Whichever way you want it, Doc."

Feyerman grinned. "If I were you, I'd take a look at what I've got in my hand before you do anything foolish."

The dog handler looked down. Feyerman was holding the muzzle of an automatic pistol half an inch away from Cullen's belly.

The two men stared at each other. Finally, Feyerman spoke. "You've done me a great service by finding this animal, Mr Cullen. Now I'll repay you with your life."

Cullen turned and walked away. One of his men tried to lift up the wounded dog, but Cullen just grabbed him by the arm. "Leave him."

"He's dying."

He gritted his teeth. "I said leave him!"

They stalked off angrily into the woods.

Dr Feyerman turned to Cathy. "You shouldn't have tried to run. You knew that you wouldn't win. Look at the unicorn, he's dying. He won't last the night."

Cathy sobbed. "Please, phone for help."

Feyerman shook his head. "You have caused me a lot of trouble, Cathy. I'm almost sorry the dogs didn't get you." He opened his bag and took out a small plastic-wrapped bundle.

Moonlight tried to kick out at the scientist, but he was far too weak to do any real damage. Feyerman knelt down beside the unicorn and opened the package. Inside was a stack of Petri dishes. He scooped up some of Moonlight's blood and resealed the dishes.

He stood up. "There. Now I have everything I want from Moonlight. I'll leave you, I think."

"Moonlight is dying!"

Feyerman shrugged. "So?"

"You have to help him! If he dies, whoever finds the body will see that he's a unicorn!"

"That doesn't matter any more. I'm not going back to Roger Brannigan. I'll go to India, I think, and continue my work there. Did you know that unicorns originally came from India?"

Cathy shook her head. She knew that the longer she could keep Feyerman talking, the more of a chance she had of stopping him.

"Well, did you know that unicorns are supposed to represent all that's good in the world?" Feyerman asked.

"They *are* good animals. Magic, too."

The scientist laughed. "Magic! Of course, the childish fantasies we told the police you were suffering from. Magic, my dear, is a joke. It's just illusion."

"Then how do you explain how Moonlight is so fast and strong? You said yourself that you couldn't understand how he grew so fast."

"That's not magic, Cathy, that's biology."

She remembered the way Moonlight had jumped the

wall in the field at Furlongs, and how he'd purified the water in the pond, but she didn't want to tell Feyerman any of that, so she said nothing.

"Moonlight will bleed to death before morning, Cathy. It won't be very pleasant. I suggest you leave here before it happens." The scientist turned and walked away.

ψ   ψ   ψ

Much later, Moonlight regained consciousness for a short time. *Cathy? What happened?*

"Feyerman was here," Cathy said. "He took samples of your blood. He wants to make some more clones."

That is probably not a bad thing, Cathy. At least then there will be more unicorns.

"Moonlight, before I rescued you from Brannigan's house, I had some very strange dreams about unicorns. You caused me to have those dreams, didn't you?"

Yes. I wanted to guide you.

"You showed me a dream in which you were fighting a large black unicorn, but that hasn't happened."

The future is never written. What you saw were only suggestions of possible futures. Dreams can be seen in many ways. The black unicorn could be taken to represent the dogs.

Cathy nodded. "What are we going to do?"

You must leave me. Go back to the town and try to find help.

"I don't want to! I want to stay here!"

There is no cloud cover, Cathy. It will be a cold night, you must have somewhere to shelter. Go, it's for the best. Come back to me in the morning.

"But Feyerman said you'll be dead before morning."

He may be right, I don't know. If you don't find somewhere out of the cold, Cathy, you could die too.

"Is there anything I can do for you before I go?"

Please, try to cover the wounds to my neck, to reduce the chance of infection.

Cathy opened her bag and took out her spare t-shirt. She soaked it in water from the bottle and cleaned the ragged wounds, then tore the t-shirt into strips, and placed them over the lacerations.

There were more cuts on Moonlight's back, but she had nothing else with which to cover them. She washed the wounds as well as she could, then kissed the unicorn gently on the forehead.

"I'll be back soon," Cathy said. "I'll get some help."

She walked away, but turned back as she reached the edge of the clearing. Moonlight lay completely still, and if it hadn't been for the light of the full moon she wouldn't have been able to see him breathing.

Ψ   Ψ   Ψ

Margaret paced the flat furiously. She hadn't slept the previous night, and was sure that she wouldn't be able to sleep tonight either. It was half-past three in the morning, and she was seriously wishing she had some sleeping pills.

She didn't know how to feel. On the one hand, Cathy was missing and it was all her fault. There was no denying that. On the other hand, however, Stephen had panicked when she told them she'd phoned the police and they were on their way over. He'd grabbed his things and run from the flat.

What was it all about? Margaret wondered. Stephen didn't seem the sort to be afraid of the police. He was just another honest businessman. True, Margaret had never really managed to find out what he actually did for a living: Stephen had always side-stepped the issue whenever she brought it up.

She knew that he owned his own company, that much was certain. After all, how else would he have so much time off? It also explained why he had to go off at odd hours. He'd told her once, after a midnight phone call, that the computer had crashed in the office and he had to go and fix it, otherwise the night shift would grind to a halt.

Her thoughts drifted from one to the other. A particularly nasty part of her mind told her that Stephen wasn't going to come back, and once again it was all Cathy's fault.

Her thoughts were interrupted by the phone. Margaret dashed across the room and grabbed it before the second ring.

"Hello?"

"Margaret O'Toole? This is Sergeant Eugene McDonald in Kilcormac, County Offaly. We have your niece here."

"Oh, thank God! Is she all right?"

"She's suffering from exhaustion, but otherwise she's

okay. We're bringing her to the local hospital."

"Okay, all right. I'll be there as soon as I can."

"I would get some rest, if I were you. Take my word for it, she's fine, she just needs to take it easy for a couple of days."

"She can rest here. I'll look after her."

The sergeant paused. "Well, to be honest, Miss O'Toole, until we can determine why she ran away from home, we can't really send her back."

Margaret bit her lip. "I see. Well, what should I do?"

"Phone everyone who knows she's missing and tell them they can stop worrying, for a start. And get some sleep. You can phone here in the morning and we'll see what happens from there."

Margaret thanked him, and put down the phone, then closed her eyes and let out a deep breath. At least that was one problem solved. If only there was some way she could get in touch with Stephen.

It had been a good weekend, and Margaret was annoyed that it had been ruined because Cathy ran away. Who does she think she is? Margaret said to herself. She thinks she can ruin my life as well as her own! I didn't ask to look after her. It wasn't my idea.

Shaking with a mixture of anger at Cathy and relief that she was all right, she went into the bathroom and splashed cold water on her face. She leant on the washbasin and gazed at her reflection.

Her eyes fell upon the pendant that Stephen had bought for her. She had been delighted with it, and had secretly taken it to the local jeweller's to see if she could get an estimate on the cost. The young man behind the counter examined the pendant and told her it was worth at least fifteen hundred pounds.

It was heavy, solid gold, engraved with a stylised "M". She took the pendant from around her neck and examined it. He *must* love me, she told herself. Why else would he buy something like this?

She turned the pendant around in her hands. Upside-down, it looked as though it was engraved with a "W". Then she looked closer.

The tiny loop which secured it to the chain seemed to have been added later. At the base of the pendant she saw two small marks where another loop had been cut away: it was originally worn the other way up.

Margaret gasped and dropped the pendant into the basin. She backed away slowly, shaking her head.

Suddenly she knew what Stephen did for a living, and why he had panicked when she told him the police were coming around. Everything he had given her had been stolen.

ψ   ψ   ψ

Sheelagh had just finished giving Shane his breakfast when the phone rang.

"Hello?"

"This is Sergeant McDonald from Kilcormac in County Offaly. I have a message for someone called Sheelagh at this number."

Sheelagh frowned. "Yes, that's me."

"Cathy Donnelly asked me to phone you, and say that everything's over now. She's fine."

Sheelagh breathed a sigh of relief. "Thank God!"

"Cathy arrived here very early this morning. She was a bit hysterical, but she insisted that it was important that we call you."

"All right, I see, thank you."

"Not at all. She said she'll phone you in a few days."

Sheelagh said goodbye and put down the phone.

Shane was sitting on the floor playing with the toy unicorn that Cathy had given him. He smiled up at her, and waved the unicorn. "Horsey!"

Sheelagh smiled at her son. "No, Shane. It's a unicorn. There's a big difference."

CHAPTER XVIII

For the first time in three days, Cathy woke up in a real bed. At first she was confused, but gradually she realised she was in a hospital.

She tried to sit up, but her head was spinning and she found she was too weak.

There was a call button on the wall, and she pressed it. Shortly a nurse appeared.

"How are you, Cathy?"

"Where am I? How did I get here?"

The nurse laughed pleasantly. "You're supposed to say 'Where am I, what happened?'"

Then Cathy remembered about Moonlight. "How long have I been here?"

"Not long. You were brought in about half-past three this morning, I think. Don't worry, though, there's nothing wrong that a few days in bed wouldn't cure."

"Moonlight, where is he?"

"Moonlight?"

"My ... horse. Is he all right?"

The nurse shook her head. "I'm sorry, I don't know. Lie back, now, and get some rest."

A young policewoman entered the room. "It's all right, nurse. I want to talk to Cathy for a few minutes."

The nurse nodded and left the room. The policewoman sat down beside the bed.

"I'm told you were pretty hysterical last night, Cathy. Can you tell me what happened?"

"There were men, and dogs. They tried to kill Moonlight, but he stopped them. He was dying when I left to get help."

"And Moonlight's your horse, isn't he?"

Cathy smiled weakly. "No, he's his own horse. I'm just his friend."

"Cathy, when you wandered into the police station last night you were talking about men with guns and knives. You've been missing since Friday night. Tell me, Cathy, were you kidnapped or attacked or something?"

Cathy shook her head.

"Did something bad happen at home, or at school, that made you run away?"

"No, nothing like that. I had to rescue Moonlight."

"Okay, tell me about Moonlight."

Cathy didn't really know where to start. She knew the policewoman wouldn't believe her if she said that Moonlight was a unicorn.

"Now, a lot of what you said last night didn't make much sense, but you gave us your aunt's phone number. We had you listed as a missing person, but no-one knows how you managed to get all the way here."

"Moonlight carried me. He's a strong horse."

The policewoman took a deep breath. "Cathy, after you came into the station, the sergeant sent out three men to check the woods. There was no sign of any horse."

"You don't believe me!"

"And you also said last night that Moonlight was a unicorn."

Cathy paused. She couldn't remember entering the police station, so she'd no idea what else she might have told them.

"Okay," she said. "It's time for the whole story. You don't have to believe me, but it's true."

It took Cathy over an hour to tell the policewoman her story. She started with the frozen animal in the Norwegian glacier, told her about Lowlands and how Damian Corscadden had taught her to drive. She told the policewoman all about Roger Brannigan and Dr Emil Feyerman.

When she told of how she rescued Moonlight from the stable at Furlongs, the policewoman nodded and checked her notebook. She excused herself for a few minutes, and returned to hear the rest of the story.

ψ   ψ   ψ

Roger Brannigan staggered down to the door in his dressing gown. There were three policemen waiting on the porch.

"Mr Brannigan? We'd like to have a word with you, if we may."

Brannigan's mouth had suddenly gone dry. He swallowed. "Certainly. What can I do for you?"

"We have received certain allegations that you were involved in the mistreatment of one of your animals. A horse, I believe."

Brannigan relaxed. He was on safe ground here. He knew that his lawyers could get him off a trivial charge like animal cruelty.

"What's more," the policeman said, "we have several statements from some of your employees that you've been involved in some sort of genetic experiments."

"I'm sure that's not illegal," Brannigan said. "And that's not an admission, because I've never been involved in anything like that."

"Perhaps not, that's for a court of moral ethics to decide, but a Dr Emil Feyerman has told us that he has discovered that the genetic material from which you worked was stolen from a laboratory in Norway. He claims to have evidence to back this up. He's willing to testify in court."

Brannigan began to feel cold. "I have no idea what you're talking about."

"Furthermore, with regard to a break-in last Saturday at this house, we have reason to believe that you knew the identity of the girl involved. That is withholding evidence, Mr Brannigan. A very serious charge."

"Exactly what do you want? Or have you just come here to tell me about crimes that I'm not involved in?"

"If you continue to deny these charges, that can be

taken as resisting arrest. Get dressed, Mr Brannigan. I'd like to have a little chat with you down at the station."

ψ   ψ   ψ

"Your aunt has been informed that you're all right, Cathy," the policewoman said. "She was very worried. In fact, she blames herself for everything."

"When can I go home?" Cathy asked.

"Later today, if you feel up to it."

"Will you do me a favour first?"

"If I can. What is it?"

"I want to go to the forest, and try and find Moonlight. Will you take me?"

The policewoman paused, then nodded. "I'm sure that'll be all right."

Cathy climbed out of bed and started to get dressed. "Maybe he's still there. Maybe the policemen couldn't find him last night. They might have been looking in the wrong place."

The young policewoman nodded, but she was sure that Moonlight – if his wounds were as bad as Cathy had said – would be dead.

ψ   ψ   ψ

"It was somewhere around here," Cathy said as they marched through the forest. "It was dark when we got here, everything looks different in the daylight."

Through the trees Cathy spotted the top of the rocky outcrop under which they had sheltered.

She dashed ahead, the policewoman hurrying to keep up.

Cathy ran into the clearing, and stopped short. Moonlight was gone.

Tears rolled down her cheeks as she staggered around the clearing, searching for some clue. Everything was gone. Moonlight, her bag, even the dogs. There was no evidence that the unicorn had ever been there.

CHAPTER XIX

"They've taken him!" Cathy cried. "Those men, the ones who had the dogs! They've taken him, like they told Dr Feyerman they would!"

She had a sudden thought. "Moonlight managed to beat off the dogs, two of them were killed and one was badly wounded. Their bodies should be around here somewhere, then you'll know I'm not making this up." She began to search frantically through the undergrowth.

They found nothing.

"Cathy," the policewoman said, "sometimes, when we're under a great strain, we imagine things. Our minds play tricks on us, and we lose track of what's real and what's imagination."

Cathy shook her head. "No, that's not what happened. How do you explain how I got here, in that case?"

"I don't know. But I do know that you've spent several nights out in the cold, and I know you missed Moonlight when you left Furlongs."

"So you think I imagined everything. You think that I'm going mad."

The policewoman sighed. She knew that Cathy was

telling the truth about rescuing Moonlight, and there had been the reports from the two policemen who had seen her at Furlongs. They had said that Moonlight was a unicorn. The policewoman was sure that Cathy *thought* she was telling the truth, but she wanted to be sure that Cathy wasn't suffering from hallucinations brought on by exhaustion and starvation

"Look," Cathy said. "See? The grass is all crushed here, that's where I left Moonlight. Those men must have come back and taken him."

"And taken everything else as well?"

"Why not? They said to Feyerman that they could sell the story to the papers, and they could take Moonlight as proof. Maybe they didn't want anything left here to show that they'd hunted him down with dogs. And they were annoyed when they discovered that I was with Moonlight, they'd been given the impression that he was stolen by horse thieves. They wouldn't want anyone to know that I could have been torn apart by the dogs, so they took my bag."

"I admit that's possible. But what about the blood? You said that Moonlight was very badly injured. There should be some of his blood around here."

Cathy looked around, and shrugged. "And the dogs as well. Moonlight killed one of them by stabbing it with his horn."

"Well, look, we'll get you back home first. We have Mr Brannigan for questioning in Dunlavin. We'll see what he tells us."

ψ   ψ   ψ

The sergeant walked into the interview room carrying a sheaf of pages. He gazed at them for a few moments, then looked up at Brannigan. "Well, it seems that your lawyers have done a very good job, Mr Brannigan. They've managed to get most of these charges dropped."

Brannigan smiled. "And why not? I've done nothing wrong."

The sergeant just shrugged. "Between you and me, Brannigan, I know you're guilty. And I'll be watching you. One small slip, and you're going inside."

"Are you threatening me, Sergeant?"

"No. I'm warning you."

"Then let me warn you. I've got a lot of money tied up in this experiment, and if anything goes wrong because of police interference, I'll have my lawyers sue the police department for everything they.can get."

"Is that so? Now let me give *you* a further warning. I've had one of the lads in the fraud squad check you out. They haven't finished their investigations yet, but it looks very much as though in the past seven years you have declared less than a third of your income. You realise what that means?"

Brannigan nodded slowly.

"Good. Now, it'll be another few days before they complete their investigations. I suggest you get in touch with your accountant and try to pay back the money before you find a dozen Special Branch men knocking down your door." He put the pages into a folder, and opened the door. "Well, good day, Mr Brannigan. I hope we don't have to meet again in such circumstances."

Shaking slightly, Roger Brannigan turned and left the police station.

Ψ   Ψ   Ψ

Cathy phoned Margaret when she returned to the police station. Margaret was in a funny sort of mood, and Cathy couldn't recognise it at first, until she realised that her aunt had missed her.

"Stephen's gone," Margaret said. "He's not coming back."

"What happened?" Cathy asked.

"It's a long story. Look, when are you coming home?"

"They said I can go back today. But ..."

Margaret paused. "But what?"

"But I'm not sure if I want to."

"Cathy, don't worry. Everything will be just like it was before."

"That's what I'm afraid of. Let's be honest, Margaret. You're a bully, and right now I don't want to go back to being someone you can push around. If I go back to the flat, things will be different. We're going to be equals. Right?"

"Cathy, I don't understand! This isn't like you ..."

"We need to have a long talk. I'll see you later." She hung up the phone and turned to the policewoman. "How was that?"

The young policewoman grinned and nodded. "That's telling her!"

Cathy smiled. "I haven't even started yet."

ψ   ψ   ψ

"Maybe it *was* all my imagination," Cathy said as they walked to the bus. "When I think of it, everything was like a dream. Getting captured, escaping. The stories Moonlight told me, purifying the water at the pond. Even the dogs. It could all have been a dream."

"If it's any consolation, Cathy, the two policemen who investigated the break-in at Mr Brannigan's house have said that Moonlight had a golden horn."

Cathy stopped. "Then you *do* believe me."

"I've never believed in magic, Cathy, nor unicorns, but there's no reason to think that you're lying. Let's just say that I believe Moonlight had a golden horn – call him a unicorn if you like – but I don't believe that he was magical."

"He was. I wonder what happened? I mean, did those men come and take his body away?"

"They sound like a pretty ruthless bunch. It's possible that they want to sell Moonlight's body to the highest bidder. I'm sure there are a lot of people who'd pay a fortune to have a genuine stuffed unicorn in their sitting-room." The policewoman paused. "I'm sorry, that was a tasteless thing to say."

Cathy shrugged. "Don't worry. I know what you mean.

The thing is, Moonlight said that magic is always there. It can't be created or destroyed. Maybe some of his magic has been left behind. Maybe one day there'll be another unicorn."

"Looking at it from the magical point of view, that would be possible."

"Dr Feyerman took the blood samples from Moonlight," Cathy said. "He told me that he'd be able to reconstruct a new unicorn from Moonlight's DNA." She stopped walking. "That's it. That's what's going to happen."

The policewoman stopped and looked back at Cathy.

"So that's it," Cathy continued. "There *will* be more unicorns. Loads more. Feyerman won't want to chance having only one, in case the same thing happens. Who knows? In years to come there could be hundreds!"

"Thousands!" The policewoman said.

Cathy smiled. "One day, there could be millions!" She took a deep breath. "For Moonlight it's all over, but he did a lot of good while he was here."

"In what way?"

"Well, for a start he got me out of the house!" Cathy laughed. "Seriously, Moonlight gave me something I haven't had in a long time. Friendship."

"And confidence. Don't forget that."

"You're right," Cathy said. She turned back and looked out over the fields. "Goodbye, Moonlight."

A single tear rolled down Cathy's cheek, but she brushed it away and walked faster to catch up with the policewoman. For the first time, she felt as though her life had a meaning.

It was something Moonlight had been trying to tell her, but she hadn't really understood it until now. It had been when she went to Dunlavin to rescue Moonlight. She had asked him why he had chosen her.

You were there when I was born. You loved me and helped me when I needed someone. You are a good, innocent person, Cathy. I could have asked for no better.

EPILOGUE

Many years later, a council worker digging a ditch through what had once been a small forest came across the skeleton of a dog. Unsure of what to do, he contacted the local vet, in the hope that he might shed some light on what had happened.

Between them, the council worker and the vet uncovered the graves of two more dogs. All were Rottweilers, and had died from severe injuries.

"Look at this one," the vet said. "His chest was pierced by something incredibly strong. It went right through his body."

The council worker shook his head. "There's definitely something weird here. Look at these marks in the ground under the body."

The vet examined the marks. "If I didn't know better, I'd say these dogs had been buried by a horse." He laughed. "Absurd, really, but these look like hoof-prints."

ψ   ψ   ψ

The Wicklow mountains were a good place in which to live. Moonlight basked in the morning sun and remembered the time, many years ago, when Cathy had cured her injuries in the same pond that lay in front of him.

Occasionally he still felt slight twinges of pain from his old wounds, but they didn't bother him much. There was a series of scars on his back and throat, visible even through his pure white coat. He knew that he could have removed the scars, but he kept them as a reminder.

He turned at a rustling noise behind him. An old brown mare walked over and lay down beside him. She nuzzled against Moonlight. In the years since he had rescued her from a cruel farmer, they had grown to love each other.

There was a sudden splash as something landed in the water on the far side of the pond, then another splash, then a third.

The young unicorns played for a while in the pure water, then, growing tired, they left the pond and went to sleep by their father.

Moonlight closed his eyes. It would be a long time before the balance of unicorns and humans was restored, but he didn't mind.

For now, he was happy.

OTHER WORLD SERIES

OCTOBER MOON

Michael Scott

Rachel Stone and her family are scared by weird happenings at their stables in Kildare. But is it the locals trying to get rid of them or something more sinister?

GEMINI GAME

Michael Scott

BJ and Liz O'Connor are gamemakers, but when their virtual reality computer game *Night's Castle* develops a bug, they risk their lives to try to solve the problem. An exciting futuristic novel.

HOUSE OF THE DEAD

Michael Scott

Something goes very wrong when Claire and Patrick go to Newgrange on their school tour. Can they find a way to keep the evil powers they have released from destroying the whole of Ireland?